Hello,

Thank you for taking the time to purchase and read this book.

Before I send you on your merry way to enjoy the final Stog adventure, could I please request upon completing this story if you could leave a review or recommendation on the Amazon page.

Reviews and recommendations are a fantastic way to get writers stories out to as many people as possible and are greatly appreciated.

I would like to thank any of you who have taken the time to read any work that I have previously done or any that may come out in the future!

Hugh Barnett

In loving memory of Mark Barnett,
We always joked that the first "proper" book I ever published
would be dedicated to you.

For Brooke, Jackie, Bernice and Mum

THE STOG'S
STUPENDOUS TALE OF GREATNESS

INTRODUCTION

Dear reader,

First, if you have read two previous books about the Stog then I must commend you on your determination. It would appear at this point that there is no amount of begging or pleading that will keep you away from these bizarre and adventurous creatures!

Secondly, I would like to congratulate you on your purchase of *"The Stog's Stupendous Tale of Greatness"* and commend you on your impeccable taste in books! I can already tell that you're going to enjoy it. It's not one of those soppy *"lovey dovey"* books that your mother has been swanning over. Nor is it that horror book that your father enjoys so much about the killer clown. No, this book is for you and you alone!

It's got something for everyone:

Do you like pirates? We have that! **<u>Singing pirates actually!</u>**

Are you more inclined towards Fairy Tales that were read to you as a small child? Guess what? We have that to!

Did you ever want to read about a chicken and a rabbit having a fight? Look no further a few chapters into this book!

See, **everything!**

Now before we go any further, I do suppose that there will be some of you that have picked up this book with no idea what a Stog is. So, I guess that that is something that we will have to rectify before we move along.

Below is picture of what a Stog looks like:

Now, I am fully aware that you can't really tell from the picture above. However, every Stog is a bogey green colour (yes, they were thrilled with that description as well) except for their fluffy stomach of fur. Every Stog has a different fur colour. We don't know why and it's not something that has ever been questioned. They are noisy creatures (thanks to the trumpet like noses and antennas on top of their heads).

They are also very messy creatures! **Remember when you tidied your room yesterday?** Followed by relaxing upon the sofa to get a rest - and before you knew it - your parents went towards your room and demanded that you tidied it up AGAIN! You hadn't even been there. It was as if someone had broken into your room, made all that mess and then left you to take the blame for it. The likelihood is that it was a Stog who did that!

They love to play with your toys but more importantly **they love to eat food!** Cheese burgers, pizza, chips, crisps, sausages, bacon, kebabs, haggis, black pudding, white pudding, red pudding, bread and butter pudding, rice pudding, Stog pudding etc. They love all of that! *(No, Stog pudding is not made of Stog's. What a ridiculous assumption!)*

Now that you have a brief introduction to what a Stog is, we should maybe meet some of the key players in this book:

First, we have the Stog and his wife! These will be the heroes of our tale. There are two stories previously written about them. Although, when those stories were written children were younger. As those children have grown older so have the Stog's and (after much deliberation) it was decided that they should have their own feature length book rather than a third short picture book … There may or may not have been a time when something along those lines would have been a Christmas book entitled "Christmas Stoggings." But I digress:

The next person that I'm going to introduce to you is a young boy called Billy. He's the secondary hero of our tale who will become involved with the Stogs' lives. The opening chapter of the story will cover much more on Billy and there is little need for me to delve any further in him now. So, I will simply let you look upon the picture below:

Following on is the villain of our story. This is Warden James Hook. You may know him from other stories as the murderous, treacherous and blood thirsty captain of a pirate ship! Well, after some time of never really succeeding in that line of work; he decided it was time to follow a new career path. After some years of service in the King's Navy he was recruited as the head operator under a secret Government project. He really made a successful career for himself. But if everything were that simple then we wouldn't have a villain for our story, would we?

There will be several other characters that are introduced to you throughout our story. However - due to a tired sketching hand - I'm not going to give you animations of them all! This will give you the chance to imagine how obnoxious, kind-hearted, stupid, loving, greedy or nice each of those characters are!

With that in mind, there's nothing really left for us to do except get on with the story. So, we only have a few final things to check before we strap in for the biggest adventure that the Stog's have had yet!

- *Have you brushed your teeth?*

- *Are you settled and comfy?*
- *Refreshments are available in the lobby!*
- *Please ensure that you keep your phones on silent!*

And ...

- NO SLEEPING IN THE CHEAP SEATS!

Good, now please turn your eyes to the first chapter of the book aptly titled ...

CHAPTER ONE

Billy Thomas was small for his age. Although that didn't stop him from being as adventurous as he could. To Billy, a tablet was - *now how do I say this in a nice way?* - something that was found in a medicine cabinet for when people got sick! Alternatively, an item that a doctor would give you if you were feeling sick! *(Something for you to think about kids!)* Never was there a day come sun, rain, wind or snow that the lad wasn't outside trying to find something magical and adventurous to do.

You know those sticks you walked past earlier that had fallen out that tree? Billy would have taken those and began building a little hotel for ants to go to when they wanted to relax just so that he had something to do. Bill's parents often left the house due to work and other commitments meaning that he mainly stayed on his own. Billy could not complain about that at all. He was quite happy to roam the outdoors and look for new things to do. This was most likely because every other child in his street was BEING BORING LAYING INSIDE THEIR LIVING ROOM WITH THEIR EYES GLUED TO A TABLET!

Billy's village was roughly ten miles either side from any town and was rather remote in its miscellaneous activities for children. Although there was....

- *The swing park with only one swing that had one of its chains snapped off.*
- *The duck pond that had become home to a duck eating squirrel!*
- *The "woods" that contained no more or less than twenty trees. Three quarters of then were unclimbable due to rot whilst the others were newly planted and too small.*
- *One shop that was a vegetable shop.... (Billy's greatest hate!)*
- *Oh! And there was a pet store! But we'll get to that later!*

Yup, it was surely one of the most boring places that you could have lived and yet Billy somehow managed to make it work. He was one of the nicest boys that you could ever read about. He was brave, kind and selfless. There was just one thing missing, a friend!

Now there were classmates in his school that could have been potential friends. Let's go through the list of those pupils in his class (a class of four! I can't stress this enough it was a very small and remote village that people did not like to live in) and you can decide for yourself whether you would have wanted to be friends with them:

First, there's Grrr Lee.

I don't know why on earth the Lee parents would have wanted to name their child *"Grr"*. Perhaps they were looking for a name that wasn't that hard to spell. What they ended up happening was having a child who went through all of their lives answering an attendance register to **_"girly"_**. Which is maybe not the best thing to call someone who weighs over 200 pounds at the ripe age of 9 with an addiction for wrestling and battered Mars bars followed by three pints of full fat Coke. Layers of fat rolled over his body and his face looked like dough before its made into delicacies like cake or bread. That lad may as well have gone into any fast food takeaway and said "*good day sir, I'll have a heart attack in a tray please followed by diabetes for the rest of my natural life!*"

What I'm getting at is that that kid was fat! So fat, that he struggled to walk through doors! That every time he ran, he would take approximately five steps and be out of breath! Richter scales could have been measured mini earthquakes every time he took a step!

Grrr was also quite a nasty child. If he wasn't getting his way - or if he was bored - then he would take that frustration out on Billy. They were the only two boys in the class. Billy had come home a few times after being threatened by Grr Lee. Although, he would have never been able to catch him!

Nope, Grrr Lee was about as far away from anything in the qualities that Billy was looking for in a friend!

Secondly, there was Princess. Sounds like nice name, doesn't it? The type of name that you've maybe read about in fairy tales where a young woman was protagonist. Well, I have bad news for you boys and girls. This type of "Princess" was maybe better off serving a life sentence in a children's home where they locked the door and threw away the key!

Actually, why would you throw away the key? Someone would be able to go get it and then the possibility arises of letting Princess back out! Have you ever even tried to throw a key? You'd maybe get it ten, twenty, maybe even forty metres at away from you. What was the point in even throwing it?

Now, I should be at least fair. Princess is a nice enough girl – perhaps even a great girl - if you get on her good side. That was just the thing. It didn't appear to anyone that she had a good side! So that's how we're going to have to introduce the spoilt little princess in our story (who just happens to have the name Princess)!

She was a simple-minded, spoilt brat who had everything paid for by the endless wallet of "dear sweet Daddy." She had the newest of everything (months before it was even out) and - I'm very certain this - she had never heard the word _**"NO"**_ before. In fact, if it was ever said to her then I'm sure she would laugh it off (with that fake laugh that sometimes posh people do) and then attempt to embarrass the person who had said the word with "actually I think that it's pronounced ""*nose*"".

She was further away from being on Billy's potential friend list than fatty, earthquake boy Grr Lee ever was!

Last but certainly not least, was dear sweet
"Sunshine". Sunshine had been born into a family who did
not own a house but drove around and lived in their very
own a motorhome. She was named after the first thing that
her mother and father ever saw after she was born...

(I mean let's all just be thankful that the first thing
that they saw wasn't dog droppings. I do not think this
paragraph would have made it into the book. Not to mention,
they would have been truly awful parents!)

Although Sunshine was nice, she was still very
disinterested in Billy. She was very smart and had no time for
anyone who did not have an IQ as high as hers. Her parents

did not believe in electricity and tended to wash in any ponds or rivers that they could find. As such, Summer had a particularly funny smell about her.

Have you remembered all those names? We'll go through them **one more** time as a reminder. Grr Lee *(I'm sorry I keep writing the full name - I was very proud of myself when I wrote that name for the first time),* Princess and Sunshine. Have you got them in your memory well and truly? Good!

Now forget about them because you're never going to hear about them again throughout the whole story! They're not important in the story at all! It was simply to symbolise that you knew that Billy could not possibly have been friends with any of these people whatsoever and - as such - finds us in the predicament that he is currently in...

I guess that's a bit harsh. You did just spend all this time reading about them. Okay, they can show up later in the story. It won't be a huge part, but I do promise that they will show up later in the story.

CHAPTER TWO

Okay, so we've officially completed the first official chapter of the book!

Can you believe it?

Not one mention of the Stog?

Why on earth would someone writing a book about the Stog's *"Stupendous Tale of Greatness"* go through all the trouble of coming up with:

      A.   A fantastic title that you're not likely to forget in a hurry!

      B.   Tease all those children who are expecting a tale of a little green creature and not include him in the first chapter of the story?

All we've had so far is some boy who will obviously meet up with them as the story continues. You must already know that because it was written in the introduction! Why on earth tell such a story from his point of view. Especially when it's extremely clear that the main characters of the story are going to be those little fuzz ball green creatures that you may have already come to know and love? It just seems ridiculous!

I am also aware that you're expecting to continue this chapter in a hope that either the Stog or his wife are going to appear! Then we can get to the good stuff. I am sorry to say that I do have some terrible news for you.

They'll fully be immersed in the next chapter, I promise. But we must get there first! So, let's carry on!

You want me to say their names again, don't you? So that these first couple of chapters don't seem like such a waste of your time? Don't you worry kids, I've got you covered.

Stog!

Stog.

Stog. Stog

Stog. Stog. Stog.

Stog. Stog.

Stog. Stog. Stog.

Stog!

Hopefully that will that keep you happy for a little while.

Anyway, Billy lived in a bungalow cottage on *"Langweilig Street"*. He knew that the name of the street was something in German but did not have a tablet or WiFi of his own to work out what it meant.

But you do. Don't you reader?

You don't!

Why don't you go and find out what it meant?

No, I'm being completely serious.

Go and find out what "langweilig" means!

I promise you, I am not going to carry on the story up until you do.

You're just wasting your own time now!

Have you done it yet?

All the cottages on the street were completely identical. An exterior of bland grey bricks and slanted black tiled roofs. The gardens were all artificial grass trimmed to the same length and not a strand out of place. Even every car on the drive was of the same make (Fiesta's must have been on some crazy sale at one time) and were all dark and mundane colours ranging from "slate grey" to "mare go grey". There was little atmosphere on the street.

In fact, there was once a tale that a tumbleweed was making its way towards the street. Then it turned 180 degrees and blew off in the opposite direction because it was so appalled at the lack of appeal that the street had.

Billy lived in the bungalow with his mother and father. Mother Thomas was a night porter at the local hotel and saw Billy once a day when it was teatime. She was a prim and proper woman who believed that children should be seen and not heard. Whenever Billy asked her a question at dinner time - something as simple as asking how she had getting on at work the previous evening - she would answer by slightly stabbing him in the arm with her fork before continuing with eating her meal. I know how awful that sounds but Billy had a tremendous amount of respect and admiration for his mother. He knew that she was tired and that all the hours that she worked was to keep food on the table and to keep her family clothed.

Billy's father was a completely different kettle of fish. Mr Thomas did not have a traditional job and it had been that way for as long as Billy could remember. Mr Thomas had an amazing talent of being able to impersonate any character that you could think of. Seriously, that's how he made money for the family!

- The cartoon sailor duck
- The laughing clown villain from the comics
- Even the good and bad versions of the interchangeable character from those *"Lord of the Tiny Circular Objects that go on your fingers"* books that you've seen on the book shelf

Mr Thomas could do them all. People from the farthest towns had heard of his skills and paid him petty cash to ring him on their child's birthdays so that they could speak to their cartoon heroes. Christmas was a particularly profitable time as all the children wanted to speak with Father Christmas. Mr Thomas had a dream of being on the radio or doing audio books but just hadn't managed to catch his big break yet. He watched over Billy when his mother was at work.

Billy loved both of his parents and wouldn't change a thing about them. They were both very keen to keep him from the evils of technology and had agreed to never give him a tablet or a phone until he was old enough to need one and could spend his childhood adventuring or simply playing outside.

*Note: Dear parents, I know that your c
now distraught with the idea of not having technology
to play the newest sensation of game. I apologise for the
inconvenience. Please remind them that this is a story. A
piece of fictional work and not to worry. Please also reassure
them that I'm sure there's no child out there in this day and
age who hasn't succumbed to making their own zombie like
faces that they make whilst looking at a tablet or phone
screen.*

Billy wouldn't have had it any other way. Whilst other children's money was blown on silly games for their tablets, he was saving his money for the one thing that he wanted more than anything else.

When he had finished his dinner one evening, his mother and father called him in to the living room. They understood that he had been feeling rather lonely and had decided that perhaps now was the time that he could take upon some more responsibility on his own. They knew that he had been saving his pocket money for a pet and decided that because he had been so good over the last few weeks that they would ease his suffering and gave him a fully crisp fifty pound note.

Filthy stinking rich! That's how Billy felt as he skipped along to the pet store with his father the next morning. He wasn't sure what he was going to buy but he was certain of the following things

- It was going to be *BIG*

- It was going to be *SCALY*
- It was going to have great, big, giant *SHARP TEETH*

Basically... It was going to be a SNAKE!

He had always wanted a snake and he was finally on his way to getting one!

Billy and his father walked into the pet store that was owned by Mr Pets. That's correct the store was called *"Mr Pets' Pet Store"*. Isn't coming up with original names for different things fun?

Mr Pets was slightly older than Mr Thomas. He had thin greying hair and a gentle face that was beginning to wrinkle particularly under his sky, blue eyes. His eyes his behind half mooned spectacles. He wore a wool jumper and faded jeans. He had a kind smile on his face most of the time although he smelled as bad as his shop did.

There were all sorts of animals there ranging from goldfish to rabbits to turtles.

"Go have a look son" Mr Thomas smiled his son. "I'm going to speak to Mr Pets about possibly doing a radio advert for him."

The shop wasn't very big although it was like a wonderland to Billy. His eyes widened in delight as he explored the wonders of the store. He wondered past the glass cubicles that many of the animals were behind. Each of them looked back at him in a hope that they would be picked and brought home.

Billy looked above the tanks to see the labels of the many things that were inside and made his way towards his dream pet. The signs that he read as he made his way there were the following

- *White mice*
- *Grey mice*
- *White and Grey Mice*
- *Cheese Eating Mice*
- *Lactose Intolerant Mice*
- *Stick Insects*
- *Insects That Don't Look Like Sticks*
- *Jelly Fish (Not Made of Actual Jelly)*
- *Goldfish*
- *Other Fish That Aren't Gold*
- *Bunnies*
- *Wide Mouthed Tree Frogs*
- *Thin Mouthed Tree Frogs*
- *Hamsters*
- *Gerbils*
- *Hamsters and Gerbils*
- *Snake (DO NOT LET EAT HAMSTERS AND GERBILS)*
- *Tarantula*
- *Lizard*

Billy made his way eyes wide to the tank that was labelled *"SNAKE"*. He was so excited to see it and to take it home with him. It was a little higher than he was. So high infact, that he had to stretch in his tip toes to see clearly. He pressed his face against the glance in desperate anticipation. As he looked into the tank, he saw two humongous eyes look back at him. The creature inside the tank was not a snake. It was a small round creature with a huge nose and a fat round belly covered in purple fur. It had three buck teeth and tiny little hands pressed against the glass as it looked back at Billy.

It was the ugliest looking frog that Billy had ever seen!

CHAPTER THREE

There's a technique that you sometimes find in books - and can question the reliability of a story – where the writer does not write in chronological order. For the younger readers, that sometimes means that stories are not told in the order that events happened. For this chapter to work, we're going to have to imagine that these events took place the night before Billy went to buy his snake.

Since it's been a couple of chapters since you delved your heads into the last Stog book, you might not remember how it ends. Fortunately, this writer always has your best interest at hearts and we're going to begin this chapter with a loving mother reading those final lines – to her daughter as a bedtime story – so that this can all start to make sense.

"There'll be no use in crying, nor trying to plead of to beg.
Because the next time the Stogs bring three smaller eggs!"

As the final words were read from mother to daughter the book was closed for another night. With that, the world of the Stog's was placed into the child's bookshelf along with some of their other favourite bedtime stories. The child's mother kissed their sleeping child's head and wished them good night before slowly walking out of the bedroom and leaving the door only slightly ajar. Footsteps could faintly be heard descending down the stairs and the child's room remained quiet. The only sound that could be heard from the room was the sweet and innocent snores of a four-year-old little girl in a deep sleep.

And now children, we've finally arrived at the moment that you have all been waiting for!

Now, I don't want you to go thinking that this happens with every story book after you have fallen asleep. You must remember that this is a story. To get from this child's bedroom to the end of the last chapter requires a little bit of imagination. So, let's just say (for arguments sake) that the book placed upon the bookshelf – Entitled "The Stog's Wife" (available in digital copy) – was a "magic book." The only one of its kind!

Well, the book *"magically"* fell from the bookshelf and landed on the floor as soft as a fluttering feather. It made no sound as the pages of the book gracefully flicked through as if it were gently being blown by the wind and revealed the final page of the two titular characters the Stog and the Stog's Wife. Now, we could waste some more time and give them both names such as "Herman" and "Marsha" or "Frank" and "Vivian". But to simply make things easier for the readers who have obviously adored countless hours of the two tales of the Stog well simply remain calling them:

"The Stog!"

and

"The Stog's Wife!"

As if they knew that you would be reading this book, the two characters began to move on the page.

At first it was just a blink of the eyes. Two sets of eyes blinking concurrently!
Slowly starting to move the heads slowly. Looking from left to right.
Their arms began to stretch. Their feet began to shuffle.

Before you knew it both the Stog and his Wife were running from page to page.

First, they were over at this side!

Before quickly appearing over here!

Not wanting to be bound and restricted to the pages of a child's picture book they finally summoned the strength and made their way into the real world. *In this story, whenever I say the "real world" I am of course referring to our own. I didn't want you thinking I was speaking about Jupiter or Mars!*

"Finally," the Stog remarked almost out of breath and stretching his back into all sorts of abnormal positions. "I thought we were going to be stuck like that with no further adventures forever!"

"Sweetheart," his wife countered. "You know that the life of a writer can be difficult. Maybe they just didn't have any further ideas with where they should take the development of our characters."

"Don't you remember when it was proposed that we had a story called ""Christmas Stoggings?"" the Stog argued. "That was to be our last hurrah! We didn't even get the chance to see Father Christmas! The writer took that opportunity from us!"

"I think you're being a little bit of a princess," his wife remarked.

I think that the Stog's Wife was getting her husband confused with that horrible little girl from Chapter One.

"Ssshhhh!" silenced the Stog as they both raised their ears in horror.

They both listened with unblinking eyes as they could hear the sound of footsteps ascend from below. It sounded as if the little girl's parents were going to bed. They held their breath as they heard the muffled voices from behind the door go into another bedroom and close the door behind them.

"We have to get out of here," whispered his wife. "Can you imagine what would happen if they found out that we weren't in the book anymore?"

The Stog looked around at her with high hopes. "We'd be treated like the celebrity's we were always supposed to be?"

His wife sighed and rolled her eyes as she walked back over to the book. She looked down upon the page that they had just been released from. Upon it was three patterned eggs that remained with cartoon drawn eyes appearing through various cracks. The eyes remained as still as they had on the day that they were drawn. She stared at the page disheartened.

"They're not ready to come out into the real world yet," she resolved sadly.

The Stog walked over beside her and put his short scrawny arm around her to comfort her. "They will be," he affirmed reassuringly. "Just not yet."

She smiled at him softly attempting to reassure him that she was okay. He could see that there was a sadness in her eyes. They had waited a long time now for their children to hatch and it still looked as if it was never going to happen. Although, the safest place for them was the book. Even if they had hatched then they couldn't have come out to the real world.

With that thought in mind, both of them turned from the safety that they had always known of being inside the book and basked in the glory of being out of it in a real-life bedroom. Their eyes were drawn towards the pink coloured door and their excitement began to rise. This was their chance to see what a real house was like and not be restricted to the words of their picture book. They could do whatever they wanted here and still be back in the book before the morning light started to shine through the unicorn and rainbow patterned, purple curtains.

The Stog took a deep breath and took the first step towards the door. He froze suddenly as the floor made a loud, *CCRREEEAAAAKKKKK* as his foot had tenderly placed upon it. There was a sound of disturbance from the bed behind them and their heads turned in terror as they saw the body of the little girl tossing in her bed. Thankfully, she was just getting herself more comfortable in her sleep and they both continued to tip toe towards the bedroom door. They were guided by a small light that was behind the door. They had just about arrived when the most unthinkable thing happened.

To their horror, the door swung open. The Stog turned ghost white! His Wife let out a panicked scream. Infront of them stood a giant shadow that they had never seen before. It was the first giant* that they had ever seen! Upon seeing the creatures, it screamed as loud as the Stog's Wife.

It wasn't a real giant, kids. No need for alarm. Remember the Stogs are tiny little creatures and so to them we are giants. That's right, in the Stog's eyes you would be a small giant.

The "giant" was disgusted that in his daughter's room were the two ugliest, most repulsive looking frogs that he had ever seen. They didn't even really look like real frogs.

Immediately, the Stog grabbed his wife's hand and they turned and ran. They didn't look behind them to see how quickly the giant was moving behind them. They ran straight back to the book and placed their foots upon the final page in a hope to return where they came from.

But it didn't work. They were trapped. **In the real world!**

The giant quickly left the room in a hurry. One would have almost mistaken him for being as scared as the Stogs were. There were raised voices coming from across the corridor. They must have been from the parents of the girl (who was still snoring and oblivious to what was going on).

The Stog and his wife repeated jumping on the book. Again and again and again. But they had no luck. It wasn't working. They were panicking and frantically looking from the book to the door back at the book.

"Why isn't it working?" asked his wife frantically.

The giant returned; its shadow ghastlier than it had been before. It's eyes hidden behind half-moon spectacles, reflecting the small light coming from the corridor. It moved closer towards them. It was cautious but quick. Before the Stogs could do anything, they were being thrown from the book as it was swept from under their feet. They fell on their bottoms and watched in horror as the giant slowly closed the copy of *"The Stog's Wife"* and placed carefully back into the bookshelf that it had fallen from.

"The kids!" yelled the Stog's Wife in terror as their chances of being reunited with them again dwindled.

The Stog took it upon himself to get the book back. This was his chance to prove that he still had bravery in him that could not be foundered. He took a great big breath in and charged towards the giant like a hero on a noble steed. Then he made this face and pose as he smashed against something:

The second time he ran towards the giant; he was even more confident. He even made a little charge like sound (like a trumpet) with his nose as he ran. Yet again, he ended up making the same face and pose as he had done before. The third time however, he gentle placed his arms out infront of him as far as he could to stop himself from getting hurt again. He took a few steps before he could feel a glass surface. That's when they realised that they weren't as free as they thought they had been. To their dismay, they were trapped in an upside down pint glass!

Another giant shadow followed in after the original giant. They were speaking in hushed tongues that were also muffled through the glass.

"What are they saying?" the Stog's Wife asked.

The Stog pressed his ear up to the glass and listened as well as he could. The voices weren't entirely clear, but he could make out most of what they were saying.

"What are we going to do?" came the familiar voice from outside of the glass. It was the woman's voice that they had heard countless times before.

The voice had recited "The Stog's Wife" many times to the little girl who was sleeping. It could only be presumed that this was her mother. Although they were fairly certain that she could not see them under the glass because if she had then she would have certainly been able to identify them **as Stogs and not frogs!**

The other voice wasn't as common. They had heard it once or twice before but could identify it as the girl's father. He was slightly calmer than the panic-stricken mother.

"We don't know where they've come from. There's no other option," said the second voice. "I'll take them into work with me tomorrow. Sammy could do with some different type of food."

The giant looked over at the glass and placed something underneath it so that the creatures could not escape. He placed them in a glass container and left them downstairs and alone for the night. The Stog's Wife had begun weeping. She no longer wanted an adventure and just wanted to return into their book with the kids. Although, that was not the Stog's only worry.

The name "Sammy" had been mentioned. It had also been mentioned that Sammy could do with some different food. They didn't know who or what Sammy was but neither the Stog nor his wife liked the idea very much of becoming someone's dinner.

CHAPTER FOUR

Stop panicking! We've done the set up now. You know and I know that the Stog and his Wife are okay from the ending of the last Billy Thomas chapter. There is really nothing to worry about. They are not going to be eaten by a snake!

But …. Rather than go into the gory details of what happened in *Mr Pets Pet Store* I'll just tell you this. Remember from those previous Stog stories how much that the Stog likes to eat food? Well, it turns out that the Stog likes to eat anything! Therefore, the terrifying snake isn't so terrifying because he's now been swallowed whole …. So, I guess that that is pretty much the end of this chapter.

Rather short. Wasn't it?

I really don't know what else to say about it. So, I won't! Instead, I'll give you something else. Rather like one of those adverts that comes on the television when your favourite TV show is on and all you want to do is get to the main story.

Let me set the scene. As with all great ideas, some don't ever truly come into fruition. There was once a time where you could have had something called *"The Stog Collection"* which would have included the two Stog stories already available, *"Christmas Stoggings"* and two poems relating to Easter and Halloween.

Instead, what you got was this book and (I think you'll all agree) thus far what a wonderful addition it's been to the Stog timeline. But I think we need a break from that main plot for a little while. Therefore, I've added tone of those poems for you to keep yourselves occupied with up until we get to the next chapter.

Ladies and Gentlemen – of the jury – the Stog and his Wife are very proud to present to you their Easter themed poem:

"The Battle of the Hare and Hen Tavern"

There once was a Chicken who laid eggs, you see
Cause a Chicken laying eggs is its destiny.
He was so dang happy and so darn proud,
Cause a Chicken laying eggs is what is allowed.

There also was a Rabbit whose name was Bunny,
With a surname "McRabbit", yeah it was funny.
He made eggs too but in the middle of the night,
Cause if the Chicken found out then they sure would fight!

Christmas passed and New year came,
Valentine's Day followed and all stayed the same.
But one fine day it all came to blows,
When Chickens fight Rabbits, everyone then knows.

It happened in a bar up north they say,
"The Hare and Hen Tavern" that's built up that way.
The Chicken got firey and the Rabbit got mad,
And the people placing bets all around were glad.

It happened in Spring when the sun shone bright,
It drew in a crowd who were in sheer delight.
Of a brave, brave Chicken with its full rage in sight,
And Bunny McRabbit getting ready for a fight!

"I make eggs almost every day"
That's what the brave Chicken had to say.
Before cackling laughter in an evil way,
Making him the villain in the story today.

Bunny McRabbit was not stronger than him,
And didn't look scary, he was small and thin.
The Chicken laughed hard and the Chicken laughed fast,

What the Chicken didn't know is it would be his last.

The lights blew out and dark filled the room,
There were crashes and clatter and even a great kaboom!
When the torches were lit, the crowds' mouths opened wide,
At the sight of a Chicken and Rabbit in a fight!

The Rabbit had got a few punches short and stark,
Cause Bunny ate carrots so he could see in the dark.
But when the lights lit up yet again,
The Chicken fought back and he brought the pain!

The Rabbit hit the chicken with a great big log,
The Chicken fell on its bum and landed on a Stog!
He got pushed back up and punched the Rabbit in the face,

A Chicken and Rabbit fight is a big disgrace!

The Rabbit pinched the chicken with the thorn of a rose,
The Chicken fought dirty and bit the rabbit in the nose.
The Rabbit gave the Chicken the old "one.... Three,"
Taking number two is his own tummy.

Not too long and they were both grumpy,
A Chicken and Rabbit tired and hungry.
The Rabbit gave the Chicken an egg you see,
And the Chicken ate up that chocolate delicacy.

Now from around Christmas time when you're in the shops
You'll see those eggs that passed that chickens chops
An agreement was made that the chicken would make eggs
all round
But the Rabbit's chocolate eggs of Easter were also allowed!

Wasn't that fun. Okay. Back on with the main story!

CHAPTER FIVE

Before we go any further, I do have a question for you. I would like you to think very hard before you answer. How many ideas have you ever had that went exactly to plan? I'll give you a few moments to think.

Writer starts twiddling thumbs and whistling drastically out of tune

I'm sure you came to the same outcome as I did. It's very rare if your plans go exactly the way that you hoped. The best laid plans of mice and men and all....

As you can probably gather this chapter is going to tell the tale of how the Stog's fantastic idea did not go to plan as it could have.

I do have to go into some detail though about their new captor's room. Both Stogs had heard muffled sounds as they had been taken from their previous location to this one. They had heard the name "Billy" being said a few times and could only assume that was the name of the child who had been staring at them through the glass container in the pet shop.

Billy's room was large and painted like a mustard yellow sort of colour. It had a few posters with some comic book heroes on there. The main thing that caught the Stog's attention was the number of books that they could see. It turned out that their captor must have had the biggest collection of books that they had ever seen. Some were battered and worn. Time had not been kind to them. It looked as if they were bought at a second-hand bookstore. There were a few that had fresher covers in the collection that looked as if they had been freshly bought. Although there weren't many. Most of them seemed to be by one writer who the Stogs assumed to be their captor's favourite author. They read the titles to some of the book's spines with the authors name showing as "CM VEAL".

As the Stogs came up with their spontaneous and amazing plan they kept seeing some of the book titles from the spines of the writings of Ms Veal. Here's some of the title names that stood out to them personally:

"THE STRANGE TALE OF THE MAN WITH FEET FOR HANDS"

"NO, DON'T GO THAT WAY!"

"RUB-A-DUB-DUB DUCKY!"

"FRANKENSTIEN'S MOTHER"

"I DIDN'T EVEN KNOW I WAS A BOOK!"

"IF YOU EVER SEE ME CRY"

"THE EVEN STRANGER TALE OF THE MAN WITH HANDS FOR FEET"

"I'M BEING SERIOUS, DON'T GO THAT WAY!"

"ONE DAY, I HOPE THEY MAKE ME INTO A MOVIE"

"THE GREAT OUTDOORS WITNESSED THROUGH A WINDOW"

"THE GREAT INDOORS WITNESSED THROUGH A DIFFERENT WINDOW"

"HOW MANY BOOKS DOES THIS GUY HAVE TO WRITE TO BE TAKEN SERIOUSLY?"

"THE STRANGEST TALE OF THE MAN WHO HAD HANDS FOR FEET AND FEET FOR HANDS"

"FINE, IF YOU'RE NOT GOING TO LISTEN TO ME. I'M JUST GOING TO GO THIS WAY!"

From what I have heard this last title was Billy's favourite story by the author:

"I BET THEY'RE DOWN THERE RIGHT NOW, SCREAMING UP AT US."

Billy and the Stogs haven't really had the chance to get to know each other yet. I'll let you into a little secret as well, the way that this chapter is going doesn't really add a great deal of hope that they will become great friends by the end of it either. However, I can tell you this, if I had gone into that boy's room and read some of those book titles then perhaps I'd have had at least one more friend in this world.

That didn't happen with the Stogs. They carried on with their escape plan. Which is probably a good thing because if they didn't do that then the next series of events would not have happened. Therefore, we would not have had a story. Can you imagine reading a book entitled *"The Stog's Stupendous Tales of Greatness"* and **not** have a stupendous tale of greatness? What a world that would be to live in!

To carry on within their escape plan then the Stogs needed to have just that ... A plan to escape! This is the best that they could come up with that night:

STEP 1:

Wait until their captor would open the Hatch above the tank to offer the Stogs their food.

FIG 1·Ø1

STEP 2:

Using their super ability to jump extremely high (a never mentioned before plot convenience) the Stogs would then attack their captor and tie him up. Ensuring that he could not escape and warn the other giants would be extremely important so that their plan to escape could not be thwarted!

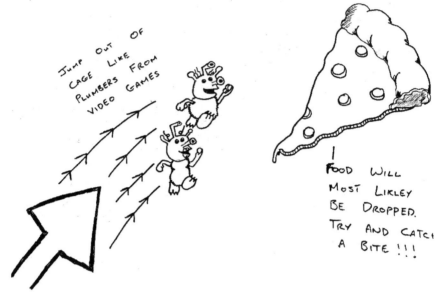

FIG 1·02

JUMP OUT OF CAGE LIKE PLUMBERS FROM VIDEO GAMES

FOOD WILL MOST LIKLEY BE DROPPED. TRY AND CATCH A BITE !!!

STEP 3:

Make their way to the books that could be found at the bottom of their captor's bed. Out of all that could have been selected, these were the thickest looking books that would be perfect for Step 5!

Fig 1·03

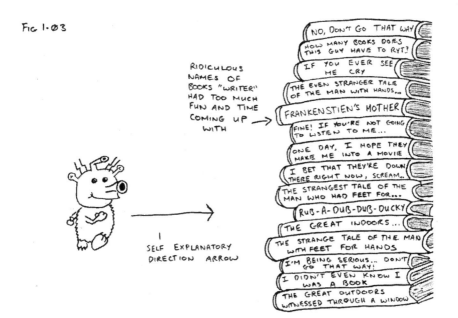

RIDICULOUS
NAMES OF
BOOKS "WRITER"
HAD TOO MUCH
FUN AND TIME
COMING UP
WITH

SELF EXPLANATORY
DIRECTION ARROW

STEP 4:

Force the tied-up captor to open the closest window

FIG 1·04

WINDOW OPEN. MAKES PLAN BETTER!

STUPID HEAD

STEP 5:

Using the thickest paper that they could find from the thickest books in the bedroom. Each of the Stogs would make a sturdy paper aeroplane. This would also be able to carry each of the Stogs weight and they would jump put to freedom and make their way back to their own book!

FiG 1·ØS

The Stogs had planned all night. Their eyes blood red and itchy from keeping them open. They recited the steps of their plan over and over. They watched – impatient at the length of time it took the boy to wake - as they waited for him to feed them. They were both hungry, starving perhaps! Even if they had not planned to escape their stomachs were growling like an untamed bear.

Finally, they watched as their captor slowly rolled out of bed that morning and shuffle towards them as if he were a zombie. Every step included an involuntary growl. They waited with great anticipation until he was right above them. His hand slowly reached towards the hatch the top of their animal cage. Their eyes widened with anticipation. They knew that if they messed up this opportunity then it was highly likely that they would not get another one. Their captor's hand finally opened the hatch...

The plan started in motion! As quickly as they could they assumed their positions...

STEP 1:

Waiting for the captor to open the hatch

Step 1 – Complete ✓

STEP 2:

With a mighty jump – as if their lives depended on it - both Stogs broke themselves free from the cage and scrambled upon on the boys striped t-shirt. It happened so quickly; they did not have time to think. Suddenly their captor did not seem scary at all. Just a scared nine-year-old boy he let out a mighty scream.

Remember when your mother saw that spider the other day? Perhaps when your teenage sister screamed when she realised that she had broken a nail? Well, the boy's scream was louder and higher than that!

An absent dressing gown tie was on the floor loose from its dressing gown. The Stog's Wife sprung free from the boy and grabbed one side of it. Both the Stog and the boy looked from each other to what she was doing; surprised at her speed. As quick as lightning, they must have both realised the situation that they were still in and returned to screaming at each other. They now sounded like there was two screaming goats in the room trying to surpass each other. The boy was so consumed in his incomprehension that he failed to notice one of his own shoes on the floor and tripped over it.

He fell to the floor sounding like the whole room was crashing around him. Luckily, Mrs Thomas had not yet returned from night shift and Mr Thomas was practicing voices down in the kitchen that morning. None of them would be able to stop the commotion that was going on upstairs.

Stog's are known for many things. Although, something that is not often recorded about them is how good they are at tying knots. If there was a **"Stog Club"** that was the equivalent to the **"Girls Brigade"** or **"Boys Brigade"**, then I can confirm is that at least every Stog would have gained a badge for tying knots. The Stog jumped off of the boy almost as quickly as his wife had. He grabbed the other side of the dressing gown tie. Together, they tied the boy's hands securely behind his back and confirmed that he could not escape. Don't believe how good they were at it? Look at the picture below. You can see for yourself!

Step 2 – Complete ✓

STEP 3:

Their eyes started to burn as sweat fell into it and they could feel their hearts pounding so fast it were as if they could burst. Yet, they made their way from the boy and straight toward the pile of books that were at the end of his bed.
There were:
Big Books,
       Little Books,
              Thick Books,
                     Skinny Books,
                           Book's that didn't want you
                      to know their weight

AND

Books that actually wanted you (and every one) else to know their weight!

There was a heavy book at the middle entitled *"WHY SHOULD I LEARN ALGEBRA? ... I'M NEVER GOING TO GO THERE!"* by M.R. Reynolds (one of the very few books that had not been written by CM Veal in the collection) that looked as if it would be perfect for creating stable paper planes. The Stog felt his chest tighten like his insides were twisting as he thought of the amount of heavy lifting to get to the book but carried on with his plan, exhausted. The Stog's Wife stayed close to the boy as the Stog began puffing and panting heavily whilst removing the books.

Step 3 - Complete ✓

STEP 4:

After a moment or two, The Stog's Wife grabbed a pencil and like one of the men on the boy's many posters brought Billy to his feet with a threatening stance. She would never have hurt him, Stog's don't threaten children of course. But at this moment in time, the boy certainly didn't need to know that.

There was some grumbling from the boy as he was pressed to make his way over to the window. It was nothing that she couldn't handle. She was more than confident that she could ensure that he would cooperate with her requests.

She waited for the boy to get to the windowsill before attaching the pencil to her back and climbing up his legs and back until she was upon his shoulder. Returning the pencil into her hands and resuming her threatening stance, she growled at him to ensure that he knew who was in charge. After a few growls (which actually sounded like the noise of a hissing cat) she mimed an order that he was to open the window.

For a moment, the boy froze. Unsure if he was able to follow through with the demand of the tiny creature. They could get hurt if they were planning on trying to get out of the house. That would have been irresponsible, especially for someone who had been requesting a pet for such a long time. The creature mimed the command again and pushed the pencil further towards his face. The point of the pencil pricked his nose a little. With uneasy tension, he reluctantly opened the window.

The Stog's Wife's eyes widened with excitement. It was like Christmas where every present was another thing that you asked for from Santa. She looked from the window back to the Stog with great anticipation and relief that the plan was almost complete!

Step 4 – Complete ✓

STEP 5:

Mr Thomas was especially excited as he excited his bedroom that morning. He had gotten up extra early that morning to have a follow up conversation with Mr Pets regarding recording a radio advert for his pet store. It would have been his first proper paid gig as a voice actor. He was over the moon with how well things seemed to be going. After some proper negotiations, he had won the role of "Fluffy".

(He was going to play the voice of a puppy on the advert, who would inform the listeners all about Mr Pets' Pet Store.)

This could be it! This could finally be his big break! Then he could also provide an actual income for the household. He may have finally had the chance to see his wife for a while (as she wouldn't have to work so much throughout the night.)

Mrs Thomas had returned home and was now sleeping in bed after working all night. There would have been no use in waking her and telling her the good news. It just wouldn't have registered with. At that point, it would have been more likely that he would have been shouted at. But he could tell Billy! He didn't think he had ever been more excited to give his own son that *"follow your dreams"* speech that he had written down years ago and kept in his wallet. Which went a little something like this:

"Son, over the years people will be more than happy to tell you that you can't do something. They'll do that because it doesn't fit in with their simple belief that "you're born, you work and you carry on like that until the end" … They've told me that many times. Time to get a real job or to stop living with your head in the clouds. But if this proves anything Billy, it's that persistence and hard work are always

the key. Never giving up on the goal that you want to achieve. Look at me, almost twelve years in and not really getting anywhere. But now starting to achieve everything that I ever wanted to with my own career. Don't ever give up Billy, if there's something that you want and you've got the urge to go and achieve it. Then you go and do just that!"

He was very proud of this speech. He was sure that he would be prouder delivering the speech than he was writing it. He swivelled towards Billy's room in an excited dance routine and opened the door with a giant

HUZAHHHH!!!!

What he found in there wasn't the overtired boy he had come to know in the mornings over the years. His good news disappeared quicker than it arrived as he stood confounded by the madness that was conjured in the room.

Billy – his own son - was tied up and being forced to open a window by his Pets! In this moment of madness and bewilderment, Mr Thomas did the only thing that his body would let him. He let out a yelp of terror!

The Stog's Wife reacted first to the surprising noise. Her feet shuffled unwillingly from below her and before she knew it, she lost her balance from Billy's shoulder. Dropping the pencil almost immediately, she grabbed for his pyjama top. Her hands were unable to grasp it as the body of the boy swayed to and fro. Horror reached into her eyes as they grew wider whilst her pupils shrank. She missed the boy entirely and fell out of the open window.

Imagine those falling shots in those epic scenes from films. You know the ones! Where the fall of a titular character is slowed down with fantastic, orchestrated music. There's one with a lion that contains a falling scene that brings tears to children's and adults' eyes alike. Even as this writer pens these words to the paper, he's welling up a little. That's how dramatic this fall was!

The drama continued from the other side of the room. If you had an orchestra in the background the tension in the music would have been unbearable.

"NOOOOOO!" screamed the Stog as he watched his beloved fall to her fate.

Mr Thomas's head turned from Billy to the other small creature at the bottom of the child's bed. He repelled in aghast upon hearing the creature speak. His legs lost all feeling and became jelly. His eyes becoming blurry and all sounds becoming distant. He fell to the ground. He had lost consciousness before his head had even touched the floor.

That's when it happened. Mr Thomas' body fell to the ground so swiftly that no one could have imagined that it had smashed against a bookshelf hit a book with his shoulder. All of these books were older ones that Billy had read; except one! Unlike the other books in the room, this one was not labelled with any fantastic title by Ms Veal. It was a story that Mr Thomas had written his son when he and his wife realised that Billy was not interested in tablets or computers. A heavy book in a thick leather binding. It shuffled a little the book from its initial touch. Although it was when Mr Thomas' body had hit the floor, the book slowly descended from the self and towards the floor. Its pages opened wide as it fell.

In a moment of shock and awe, The Stog looked up as the book fell. There was no time. He was unable to move. Frozen stiff at his appending doom. He closed his eyes tightly in terror as the book continued to fall. The book landed with a giant thud that echoed throughout the room. In a real-world scenario this would have been the death of our noble hero. But this isn't a real-world scenario. Is it kids?

*Step 5 – **Failed***

CHAPTER SIX

That children, is the end of our story. It's not the ending that the Stog or his Wife intended but alas time waits for no one.... Or fictional creature.

I'm only joking! Don't close the book! Put your rotten fruit away! Save the 1 star ratings! Could you imagine if that's how it did end though? This would have been the end all of trilogies!

No. Our story actually continues towards the darkest of seas. Thunder roaring like wild lions and rain harshly splattering against the rotting exterior of the HMS Jolly Roger. Its sails were torn and battered from the vicious attacks that the ship had barely survived in the past. It had once looked formal and inviting but now it suffered from being unrepaired, uncared for and (most of all) unrivalled. The HMS Jolly Roger was the most dangerous prisoner ship to ever sail to seas and was captained by a barbaric warden who treated his prisoners with malice and hate. A ship that no man in even the inanest of minds would want to ever enter.

Yet, this is where the Stog found himself.

Cell Block B was where the Stog had awoken after falling through incoherent colours and noises. His eyes hazy and his mouth dry, it had not taken him long to realise that he was trapped behind rusted bars in a call no bigger than a cupboard under the stairs. The bars had extremely thin gaps between them. It made it impossible for even the smallest of creatures to squeeze through and make their escape. The cell block was dimly lit by candle lanterns sporadically placed above the cells. The cell block stank of uncleaned toilets and stale rotting food.

Across from his cage there was another exactly like his. In it was a dark whimpering shadow. It sounded like a wounded animal, fragile and weeping. The Stog approached as far as he could within his own cell.

"Hello?" he called cautiously and barely loud enough so that he wouldn't be heard from the far wing of the corridor. "Hello?" he repeated, "are you okay?"

The whimpering continued and became even more fragile than it had been. It was broken by the croaking high pitched sound of someone broken and alone. "It can't ask. They'll find out," the voice spoke. "Mustn't answer. Know better"

Confused by the response, the Stog pressed his face against the bars and squinted his eyes to try and get a better look at the other prisoner. He called again, "are you okay?"

The prisoner ignored him this time. Consumed within his own imprisonment. The Stog was getting slightly angry and confused. Wherever he was, he shouldn't have been there. He needed to get back to the room and find out what had happened to his wife.

Becoming impatient, he growled as he spoke. "Where are we?" he demanded, "what's going on?"

"Shut it!" hissed a voice from the cage beside his own.

The Stog cautiously moved over to the side of the cage and looked into the darkness of the cage beside him. His footling failed him as he realised what was trapped in there and he tried to revert into his own space.

From the darkness emerged the most giant of pigs. It was tattooed from head to toe and its mouth was missing several teeth. The pig was muscular and lean. He had several scars on his face and was smoking a tobacco pipe. The Stog – further startled by the beast's hideous appearance - backed away further from the side of his cell and pressed his back up against the far. His mouth became dry. He was lost for words.

As the tobacco in the pipe ignited, the pig's eyes flared up like fire as it stared at the Stog from behind its own cell bars. There was silence for a few moments which felt like forever. At last, the pig spoke:

"Sorry if I scared you. Little fella!" it growled through its harsh voice.

Putting on a brave face, the Stog stepped forward slightly. "Scared? No, not me sir! I wasn't scared at all". Although, he could certainly feel that some of his bones were still shaking and his teeth were still chattering.

The pig howled with laughter at the remark. It was a vicious laugh that appeared to the Stog to go on for rather too long. Although he left the pig to it.

"Righteo then" the pig said a little too unconvincingly for the Stog's liking. Although it was nicer to talk to someone who was interested in talking rather than having no one to talk to.

"What's wrong with that guy?" he questioned, speaking about the prisoner he had already encountered. Immediately, he then asked his follow up question. "Where are we?"

"Mustn't ask," screeched the tainted voice from the cell across. "Mustn't answer!"

The pig looked over toward the shadows where the voice was coming from. It took another inhale of its pipe before it spoke. "Wrong?" He quizzed. "Laddie, do you not know where we are?"

The darkness from the cell across screeched in an unholy tone. Its voice was barely decipherable as its eyes came into focus from the lantern above both of their cells "Mustn't tell it! Not it's business!" it cried.

The pig ignored the creature's warnings. It chuckled slightly as it announced in a overselling welcoming tone, "You're on board the HMS Jolly Roger, of course! The most notorious and barbaric prison ship to sail the seas."

The creature wailed again whilst heavy doors slammed open from the furthest side if the corridor. The sound of thumping boots marched through them and along the corridor towards their cells as two heavy set pirates entered the corridor. Both passed many cages as they made their way along the corridor. They halted right in front of the Stog's cage. He pressed towards the back of his cage again and tried to swallow as his eyes gazed upon them. There was a lump in his throat that would not diminish. They smelled as if they had not washed in weeks and his nostril burned even this far back from them. Their gleeful smiles showed their yellow and golden teeth as their eyes widened at their new captive. Then they turned towards the opposite cage.

One unlocked it whilst the other emerged into the darkness and was joined by the pitiful wails and screams of the captured creature.

"No!" it pleaded mercifully. Each scream came across he voice across as a scream of fear and agony. "Didn't answer!" it attempted to explain as it sounded like it was being dragged from the cell. "Begged it stopped!" it wailed again as the second pirate went into the darkness and both emerged dragging a thin creature along the floor. Pale in colour and clawing at anything to try and refrain the pirates from taking it. As the Stog came close to the front of his own cage he could only see the creature's hand pitifully trying anything not to be taken through the large heavy doors at the other side of the corridor. Before the doors slammed shut behind them, he heard the final gambling and pleading scream of the creature echo through the cell. Even after they were long gone, the screeches failed to leave the Stog's ears.

The pig inhaled his pipe again as the silence overcame the cell block. "That's Hook's plaything!" he stated. "If he wants any information on anything, these days he'll usually get it out if him. Poor guy, he's just a broken replica of what he used to be. Hook took away his belief that he would never grow up. When that happens to a kid then that's when their whole world starts to change. Lost the ability to fly and all. He was always scared of growing up and being alone but most if all... Being forgotten."

CHAPTER SEVEN

Billy was horrified at his father's mishap!

I'm trying to think of the easiest way that I can to explain this. Let's look at it this way:

Would *you like a brand-new puppy?*
Then let's get you one!
Here he is!
This is Fido!

Isn't he cute?

He's got the cutest little face in the whole wide world, doesn't he?

Fido is yours to keep!

(Dear parent – I am sorry, but I need you to do this to emphasise the point - please now slam the book shut and say the following words.... FIDO IS GONE FOREVER!!!)

It took you a while to reopen that book. Was that because if the tantrums? You must have felt horrible. I am sorry but – at the same time - you are welcome. Now, everyone reading knows what it's like to be either Billy of Billy's father! Now we can simply carry on with the story.

"How could you!" Billy screamed.

Mr Thomas' eyes had just started to open. He was unsure for a moment what had happened. Slowly it was coming back to him when he realised that the heavy leather book was no longer on the bookshelf and had landed right on the spot where Billy's pet had been. For a moment he thought he was going to be sick before realising that was simply the feeling of pity for teaching his son about the brutality of life. It slowly sank in that he had caused a heartache that his son may never forgive him for. But wait!

Now children, this is especially important. Although they will deny it to you, every parent in the world knows about the magic of books. That books change every time that you read them. You go on the same adventure but realise things that you didn't notice the first or the second second or perhaps even third time that you read them. Mr Thomas had read his son a story about the boy with glasses who goes to the magic school at least three times and every time that he had he had noticed something at made him audibly pause and go, "ohhh" ....

Furthermore, Mr Thomas knew tales about animals disappearing into books. He had once had a friend on a farm who had sworn that a cow had once got into a nursery rhyme book and to this day was still jumping over a moon. Although he had never heard of a creature coming out of a book. It was impossible for him to comfort his son at this point .

Billy was so upset with his father that he grabbed the book with fury and flicked through the pages frantically. His heart sank and in a fit of anger he threw the book out of the open window and fell to his bed. He threw his head into the pillow and felt his tears land softly into it as he cried. Mr Thomas didn't know what to do. As Billy wailed into his pillow, his father slowly left the room in dismay.

CHAPTER EIGHT

Although the inside of the house was full of sorrow and regret, it was on the outside that our adventure continues.

On the outside of the window, in the middle of the mid-day sun the book landed onto the ground. Its pages opened wide open and a little higher above it - dangling with the little strength that she had left in her arms - was the Stog's Wife.

She wouldn't believe that her husband was dead. There wasn't a chance of it. She knew that her children's father and the creature that she loved was still alive. If there was anyone who was going to save him now then it was her.

She took a deep breath and closed her eyes. She had one chance at this and if she was to fail then perhaps that was the end of her story. She could feel her grip losing its strength from the window ledge. She had to get this just right. Her heart pounding and refusing to exhale. She let go of the window ledge and could feel herself falling through the air. It felt almost graceful. She felt like an angel of sorts. Fond memories flooding through her as she kept her eyes shut.

Her husband. Her eggs. The children she would soon have once they hatched. It created a sense of warmth and comfort to her. She didn't feel like she was falling. She felt like she was flying.

That continued until...

CHAPTER NINE

It had been a few hours before the pirates returned to Cell Block B. In that time the Stog had spent as much time with the pig and learning as much as he could about where he was. He had learned of the HMS Jolly Roger's purpose. The HMS Jolly Roger was a prison ship for fairy tale creatures that had been sentenced to jail. Since no ordinary jail would take mythological creatures then it had been decided by order of the Mayor of London that a fairy tale character should take control of the situation. This had been supported by the UK Government and the Royal Family.

The deed was granted to none other than the honourable Captain James Hook. He was given a newly built ship and requested to sail the seas in search of fairy tale creatures who should have been in prison a long, long time ago. He made the newspapers quite quickly when he made his first capture of a young boy who had tormented sailors on the sea with his antics. Many good pirates had been tortured by the boy and his fairy friend. None were happier than Warden Hook when the boy was captured (as he too had a debt to repay). The boy had once taken the Warden's hand (with a ticking alarm clock attached to it – of all things!) and fed it to a crocodile. It was said that the crocodile still searched for the rest of Hook after acquiring a taste for him.

The boy was now simply known as Prisoner 001 or Prisoner Pan. Hook had spent years ensuring that the boy could not escape and even broken him enough that he couldn't fly anymore. Upon the realisation that he would never escape the prison ship, Pan had become a shadow of his former self. The boy had always refused to grow up. Hook had tortured him until he had no imagination to keep his youth alive. He was now a skinny, middle aged man who time had not been kind to. He was forced to wear a torn business suit two sizes too big. His youthful body had grown full of wrinkles and had become almost become a grey like colour due to the lack of sunlight. His hair had also receded and thinned. With his spirit broken, he was now Warden Hook's prized prisoner. Proof to the UK Government that his ship and crew could break the mould of any of the characters that they captured and bend them to their will.

The Stog listened intensely to the pig as he told the stories of some of the other prisoners on the cell block:

There was a wooden puppet boy who had been accused of feeding his father to a whale. There was a tell when he lied (his nose would grow longer). When it came to his trial he must have lied so much. The Judge sent him to the prison ship after the puppet boy's nose had grown so long that it poked the him in the eye!

A little girl who had gone mad after falling down a rabbit hole and ever since had spoken of a strange and magical land that she had apparently fallen into. The civilised people of London had given her up to the authorities as they believed her to be a danger to herself and others. She had been caught trying to push herself through any rabbit holes that she found ever since.

There was a boy a few cells down who was now branded Jack the Ripper. He had chopped down a beanstalk with a mad look in his eyes a few years back. What had happened though is that he had caused an elderly giant to fall and die whilst doing it. Upon further inspection it had appeared that the boy had stolen a golden egg, a golden goose and harp from the giant. The murder of the giant had certainly been no accident!

Perhaps one of the most surprising was the tears coming from two cells across from the Stog's. It contained a young girl with jet black hair who was deeply upset that she was in prison. A wolf had eaten her grandmother and she had taken it upon herself to exact revenge on the wolf. She had once worn a red cloak that her grandmother made but she completed it with a wolf skin scarf. It had been the only evidence that connected her to the crime.

Finally, there was the pig. He didn't give too much away about his crimes before he had become a prisoner on the ship. Although, he had been placed in the cell with two brothers who were no longer with him. The only clue was that the pig would not stop eating bacon.

As the cell block door slammed open again, the pirates could be heard dragging their feet along the corridors. The corridors echoed again with the pitiful cries of the hurt Prisoner Pan. They threw the disgraced man in to his cell as he wept and crawled back into the darkest corners. His silhouette curdling into a ball. Like a frightened hedgehog. His weeps turned into slight hissing as the pirates moved from his cell.

The Stog and the pig's eyes followed them as they dragged themselves across from Prisoner Pan's cell to theirs. Both were rotund men with shirts too small for their belly's. They had long greasy hair and unwashed faces with beards still containing yesterday's dinner (cabbage soup it looked like!). They smelled worse than they looked. They ignored the pig completely and towered over the tiny little Stog. Their eyes curdled in disgust and they laughed mockingly after spitting at the Stog.

"Evening squires!" grunted the pig, interrupting their fun. "What is it that we can do for you?"

The pirate's stench of breath revolved from the Stog's cell and moved towards the pig's. His eyes started to water a little as if they were burning at the rottenness of it all. As brave as the pig had shown himself to be, the Stog could tell that he was frightened of the pirates. If anything, if the pig was afraid of the pirates... Then what chance did the Stog have?

"Boss wants to see him," sneered the first pirate.

"Yeah," jeered the second one. "Got a little friend that he thinks this little fur ball will like to meet."

Each of the prisoners from the cells pulled their faces up towards the bars of their own cells. All of them looked worried for the Stog. A shudder could be felt each of them. They knew the likelihood of the Stog never returning to the cell. They knew exactly what friend that the pirates were talking about.

"Needs to meet *Lucinda*, dun he?" growled the other pirate with a smile of vile delight on his face.

"Come on lads," protested the pig. "Leave the kid alone!"

"Shut your face!" demanded the first pirate and the room went cold and silent.

All the prisoners in their cells backed away to the walls. Prisoner Pan wailing in fear and horror as the pirate moved his head so close to the pigs at the other side of the cell door that they were practically both breathing the same air. for the first time since the Stog had been upon the ship, the pig did show some fear. His legs were shaking and his eyes were watering slightly as the pirate continued taunting him.

"Captain's been craving pork recently," escaped the words from the pirates stinking mouth. "We'd love nothing more than to feed it to him."

Both pirates wailed with horrifying and unnatural laughter. It echoed across the whole cell block and the prisoners all reacted to it differently trying to block it out. They were trapped in here. Perhaps for no other reason than being different. But the Stog would not give up. He had been in the cell for some time now. He had searched every nook and cranny to try and figure out a way to escape but here was no possible way out....

But now he could have an opportunity to find one!

"I'll go," he gulped as the pirate unlocked his cell.

The pirates laughed ferociously. As if this tiny little creature had thought that it had had a choice in the matter. The corridor was silent, but all of the eyes of the prisoners fell on the Stog as he made his way through it. As the pirates dragged themselves behind him, they ensured that the lamps behind them were dimming and chuckled a little more. The corridor door opened once more as they walked through it together and slammed behind them. Cell Block B had not been that quiet for a long time.

CHAPTER TEN

Now pirates are extraordinary types of people! I'm sure that you as the reader; have heard all sorts of things about how horrible and despicable pirates can be! But as the stog was brought from the cells above deck and escorted towards the captain's quarters he learned something about pirates that he did not know.

Pirates like to party at night-time. Not only do pirates like to party at night-time but they like to make their own songs to party to! Now I do warn you that the songs that these pirates sang is not like the songs that would be sang in some animated feature chorus. There's heavy rock guitars and big catchy choruses. It's almost like some extortionate big rock concerts are performed on those pirate ships.

Pirates sing about some of their favourite things. Rum. Beer. Mead. Treasure chests. Rocking quests and lots of other things. But if I told you everything that they sang about, then this chapter would ruin the rest of the story. But I think we have time for one of their party songs.

The song went like this:

YAHARR!!!

Not so long ago you thought of us as thieves
But now you seem to think of us as Johnny Depp or Pirate Steve
So now we must voyage pillaging the seven seas
With the splinters of my wooden leg still digging in my knees

Ye used tae fear o us (YAHARR!)
The way we used tae cuss (YAHARR!)
We were known as the mad dogs of the sea!
But now ye cause a fuss (YAHARR!)
If we don't drive a bus (YAHARR???)
It's time to make ye fear again of piracy!

So!

P
IS FOR MY "PARROT WHO CANNNAE FLY AND I CALL SQWUAK"
I
IS FOR THE "ICY SEAS THAT WE SAIL ON WHILE WE ROCK"
R

IS NOT MY FAVOURITE LETTER THAT SOME PIRATES SCREAM
TOO LOUD
A
IS FOR "AHOY MATEY THAT WE SING LOUD AND PROUD"
C
IS WHERE WE VOYAGE AND C IS FOR MY "CREW"
AND
Y
IS FOR THE "YELLLERBELLY LAND LUBBERS JUST LIKE YOU"

(Guitar solo…. This is your moment. Air guitar solo!)

Don't ye think that I don't get it cause ye know I do
What more could ye want in this sweet life than to sweep a
deck of poo
The life and times of piracy can be ever so much fun
So grab an eye patch up lad and grab your swords and guns!

We sailed along the seas (YAHARR!)
But kept on seeing trees (YAHARRR???)
Our navigators made of paper mash and glue
We've sailed for pirate quests (YAHARR!)
We've opened treasure chests (YAHARRR!!!)
Its time tae party with the pirate crew!

So
P
IS FOR A "PIRATE'S LIFE, THE ONLY LIFE FOR ME!"
I
IS FOR THE "EYEPATCH TO MAKE SURE THAT I DON'T SEE"
R
IS FOR THE "RANSACKING WERE KNOWN FOR, WHAT YA
MEAN YE HAVNAE HEARD?"
A
IS FOR "ANCHOR THAT THE SPEED FREAKS THINKS ABSURD"
C
IS FOR THE "CANNON BALLS THAT'LL SINK YER SHIPS TAE
SEA"
Y
IS FOR THE "YARHARHAR" LAUGHED BY PIRATES JUST LIKE
ME!

We are the BAD BAD PIRATES OF THE SEA!

It's a PIRATE'S LIFE for you n' me!
Raise yer TANKARDS UP for PIRACY!

The song continued to play further but the lyrics were distant that the Stog could no longer hear them as he was brought through a gigantic wooden set of doors carved with beautiful patterns.

Through the doors was instantly a warmth that he had not felt throughout his whole ordeal of being on the prison ship. It was well furnished with a long, expensive dinner table in the middle of the room with two chairs at either end of it. There were fancy candle sticks placed periodically around the room keeping it well-lit harmonising with lanterns hanging from the ceiling.

There were paintings placed around the room. They were all different canvases posed by the same figure. They were all well painted, but the figure looked repulsive! The Stog – who had been left alone by the pirates wander the room – gracefully stepped along the polished floor and did not remove his eyes from one of the paintings. The figure was presented as an angel. The ugliest angel that he had ever seen. It was as if its eyes were staring at him. Burning into his heart. He felt uneasy. It could have been the ferocity of the waves although it was unlikely. Everything about this painting told the Stog that whoever this individual was; he was not someone that he wanted to meet.

"Good evening," came a well-presented West English accent from behind him.

His body froze. He was speechless. He knew that the voice behind him was he person in the painting. The man in all the paintings. The Stog turned. He stayed in the exact point of the room. His eyes widened. His throat went dry. The paintings didn't do the voice justice. Of all the repulsive men in the world the Warden was one of them.

"So tell me," Warden James Hook began as he glared down at his newest prisoner. "How is it that that you have found your way onto my ship?"

CHAPTER ELEVEN

Kids. Let's take it back a second. I have a remarkably important question. When is the last time that you remember being so sad that you were angry? I am asking about being really, really angry!

Perhaps it was when Mum or Dad didn't let you have that extra sweet?

Maybe that time you didn't get pudding because you didn't eat your tea?

Maybe it was because you had go go to bed without any supper for not being good?

I bet when you were so angry you said or did something silly that you wish you hadn't done! How on earth would I know that? Here's a little secret ... We've all done it!

That is exactly how Billy felt when he'd calmed down. He wished that he hadn't thrown the book outside of his window and screamed at his father. He knew that his father was trying to share a happy moment with him. He had repaid him with throwing out a book that his father had once spent a lot of time on just to give Billy some joy. He had to get it back. Even more, he should probably start reading it.

He opened his door, afraid that the creak would alert his father - or his mother (who had that evening off of work) – that he was still awake as it was getting late. Not quite as late as he had stayed up before but still pretty late. He managed to sneak across the one floored corridor of the house and past the living room while his mother and father were watching the television. I don't know what it was called that they were watching but it seemed to fit in with Mum's "lovey dovey" romance stories and Dad's love of vampires. Although, he was complaining that these vampires weren't very good. Something about them shining silver!

Billy crept outside and felt very chilly almost instantly. He managed to grab the book qithout any disruptions. Slowly and carefully made his way back to his room. Every step he took made a horrendous creak. The way floorboards always tend to when you want nothing more than for them to be silent. But his mother and father never heard a thing as the television was quite loud.

When Billy got back to his room, he opened the book. He almost wished that if he had opened the book that his pet would have appeared happy and alive. There was nothing whatsoever. Except the scribblings that he had come to know so well over the years as his own fathers handwriting. Drawn away from the harsh realities of the world, Billy started to read the story that his Dad had written for him. A story he had never read before. A story of the seven seas and a mighty prison ship. It was daring and exciting and dark and something that he knew he just had to keep on
reading!

He was deeply enjoying the tale before he read about a little green creature inside a cage in a cell block! He stopped. Rubbed his eyes in disbelief to ensure that he was not reading it incorrectly. Trying to make sure that his imagination hadn't run away with him. He had become so focused on the story that he had almost forgotten what had made him go to get the book in the first place.

There had been no mention of the Stog's Wife. He was not even sure if this creature that was mentioned in the story was his pet. How could that be? Wasn't that impossible? If it was true, then what should Billy do now?

If he kept reading the story it could end with their demise **(Spoilers kids! It doesn't. Please keep reading the story!)** If it was the creature that he had had as a pet that morning, then it would be difficult to gain that creatures trust after the ordeal it had just been put through. How on earth was he going to be able to achieve that?

Then it came to him!

He just had to wait until the morning. The creature had to wait until morning. But Billy had an idea!

CHAPTER TWELVE

Waves crashed against the ship. It swerved viciously. However, the inside of the Captain's Quarters seemed somewhat calmer.

It couldn't possibly have been because of the Warden's demonising look. He had eyes like fire. Filled with intrigue and jealousy. He had long black hair and a villainous moustache. The type of moustache that only a villain would twirl in a cartoon serial. He had a solid chin and wore a white shirt tucked into long black trousers covering knee high leather boots. His left hand was replaced with a long black metallic hook. It bore the letter "L" in a shimmering gold paint. He stared at the Stog with interested desire.

"I've never seen anything remotely like you before," he remarked civilly. "What on earth could you possibly be?"

The Stog remained silent and looked from the Warden to floor. Cautiously he backed into a corner of the room. There was about as much chance of escape in this room – if not less - as there had been in the cell block below.

Hook walked closer towards him. His black hook reflecting pieces of the light from the lanterns. His position only made him look taller and more frightening.

"I do get it, you know." It was as if he was being sympathetic to the Stog's predicament. "Starting your time in this ship in that cell block. You must have heard all sorts of terrible things about me?" He put on a voice as he impersonated previous assumptions about himself. "A mad man, a Savage. Perhaps even a psychopath. But I'm here to tell you that I am none of those things."

The Warden opened himself a bottle of rum called "Black Death" and poured a glass. He walked over to the large furnished dinner table in the middle of the quarters and sat down. He gestured over to the Stog to sit on the other chair at the opposite side of the table. Upon his request the Stog did the same.

Hook took a swig of the rum and glared across the table. He started to speak in a way that made the Stog wonder if Hook had been part of a conversation that he had not been privy to.

"My father could have been anything that he wanted to be. A writer! A storyteller! An artist! He was a man who welcomed everyone into our house with long winded and exciting tales or even jokes to try and make everyone feel included and involved. He had a mouth and a tongue for well thought out and detailed stories. Perhaps the most observant eyes so that he could offer help to even the most subtle of tells of people in trouble. He could have been anything he wanted."

The Stog looked around very awkwardly around the quarters. It was like he was in a therapy session as a therapist without even knowing.

"Instead, he took the safe and mundane job to try and provide for his family. After 14 years he was let go from the safe job and we were left struggling. We did almost anything just so that we could to survive."

"And err ..." The Stog began. It would be rude at this point if he was not part of the conversation at all. ".... How do you feel about that?"

Hook sighed wearily. Almost like he had been meaning to get this off his chest for a long, long time.

"I learned a great many things from that wonderful man. Not least being you can fail at what you don't want to do and so you might as well take the chance on doing something that you love."

The lighting on the lanterns flickered in the reflection on his eyes. His voice was no longer calm, changing into something that the Stog had rarely heard in the safety of his own picture book. It was sinister and every word was spat as it escalated into a smug, condescending rant.

"So, I went to the sea. I dreamed of being a naval general but – much like my father - fearing failure I settled for mediocrity and became a scally wag. It was only after time that I got a real taste for the sea and it ...." He paused momentarily and admired at this hooked hand almost poetically. "... In return got a taste of me."

The Stog continued to sit in silence. If this was the warden's idea of torture, then he was almost certain that he would be able to push through it. But thus far, it seemed that Warden Hook was the politest and best spoken "villain" that the Stog had ever heard of.

Hook looked away from the Stog and almost sympathetically towards the hand on which his hook was on. He tittered slightly to himself.

"James Hook," he began, "That's the name that I was born with. Kind of funny if you think about it really, isn't it?"

The Stog forced an uncomfortable laugh. He was uneasy after seeing what had happened to the prisoner across from his own cell.

"I take it you saw my little project. The prisoner who seems to have the strangest fear of me. I couldn't possibly imagine why he thinks of me that way." There was a glint of sarcasm in the way that he had said those words which brought a slightly darker and fearful tone to the Stog's conversation with the Warden. "Did he tell you how I lost my hand?"

The Stog remained silent.

"Unfortunately, I lost it due to that prisoner's previous escapades. He needed to mature a little, you see. He needed to grow up. But before he did that he cut off my hand and fed it to a crocodile," Hook spoke calmly and still pleasantly. "As you can imagine, I wasn't best pleased but I had the finest of craftsmen make this for me. I call it ""Lucinda"", there's a tale there somewhere of forbidden love and broken hearts but I won't go into details. We have much further things to discuss. Such as how on earth you managed to get onto my ship?"

Hook took a drink from his glass and his eyes turned to the back of the room, he became distracted by something at the other side of the room. There was a lantern at the back of the quarters. It was flickering on and off. It caught the Stog's eye because every time that he noticed it flickered off; remarkably he could see something inside of it. It was like a firefly but bigger. Smaller than a mouse but recognisably a creature trapped in there.

It was too far away to see. But it drew his attention to another lantern and he concentrated his eyes before letting out a gasp of horror when he realised what was in there. In each lantern there were the shapes of tiny creatures that had been trapped. He had only ever heard of but had never seen a fairy. Each of the lanterns containing one with their wings fluttering around and banging against the glass to be begging to be let out. The Stog couldn't hear what they were saying but could only imagine their terror being in their own little prison cells.

Hook was making his way towards the one in the far corner. He smiled softly at what appeared to be an exhausted fairy inside the lamp. Her magic draining as she had been forced to stay so long in the lantern and bring light to the quarters. The stog thought about how Hook seemed to be caring for her as he gently took her from the lamp and spoke gently towards it. Perhaps Hook was a kind man after all and this had all been a big misunderstanding. What he had seen from Hook so far and the description he had been given from the pig were almost entirely opposite. Quite frankly he thought that the pig couldn't be further away from the truth.

But we've all been wrong before... Except - of course - if you ask your parents if they've ever been wrong. Parents are always right …. Even when they're wrong!

A dramatic change came over Hook almost in an instant. Gone was the pleasant man he had been towards the Stog within a lightning strike. He started to clench his fist so that the fairy's top half of her body could be seen struggling as it attempted to break free from him.

"Did I say it was lights out?" he growled at the fairy. It was terrified. Shaking relentlessly to break free from him as he laughed sinisterly.

He chuckled viciously and with distaste as he used his hook caress her wings. It wasn't too long before he stopped playing around and pierced it through one of the wings making it impossible for the fairy to fly.

He chuckled subtlety but gleefully at the pain it caused the fairy. "Lucinda does like to play with you disgusting little things. She likes to watch you struggle. Personally, I think that it makes the next part even more interesting."

The Stog watched frozen. He was unable to move at the horror of the diabolical deeds of the man who captained the ship. Hook lead the trapped fairy towards a mirror. He dangled the fairy from his hook as he looked at his reflection and questioned the mirror:

"Magic mirror on the wall, who is the greatest captain of them all?"

The mirror filled with smoke. All sorts of different colours started to dance inside of it. It was like a series of storm clouds brewing up inside of it. Then – like perhaps one of the biggest anti-climax's that this story may have to offer it - up like a secret compartment with a simple click. The whole mirror was a door that Hook walked through with the fairy. The Stog could not help himself. He knew that staying on the chair was probably safer. But he had to know what was happening. He had to know if he could help the fairy. He snuck down from his chair and followed Hook as fast as he could. But when he made it to the door and saw what was inside his heart sank.

He knew now why it seemed like there would be no escape. Because there wasn't. He had not noticed until he looked through the secret door but something had been bothering him about Hook's quarters. He had not seen a single book.

Every single book that was on the whole ship must have been behind this secret mirror under lock and key. Hook took out the only book that seemed to be chained up. The fairy let out a series of squeals that sounded nothing bigger than a mouse. She was determined to break away from his grip. She pursued relentlessly. Hook's mouth formed a devilish smile as he threw the book onto a small wooden table.

The book was black and red and torn and battered. On it was a white and grey picture of skull and cross bones. It was the type of book that looked like if you found in a library you would return it to the shelf and never speak of its existence again. Hook opened the book and the room seemed to drain of all colours. It was freezing. Like all the warmth and happiness of the world had been sucked out of it simply by a flick of a page. Fog formed all around whilst he placed the fairy closer and closer towards the book's pages. For such silent creatures of beauty fairies have the most horrific screams. It was over within a few seconds before the fairy disappeared from our story forever. Although, the scream would stay with the Stog for the rest of his life.

CHAPTER THIRTEEN

It was a warm and beautiful morning when the Baker awoke. He couldn't help but notice as he stretched that it was perhaps one of the best sleeps that he had had in a long time. He could not even tell how long he had been sleeping. He had been exhausted the night before making cakes for parties. It was a simple and yet rewarding job. He had tried his hand at being a butcher and even a candlestick maker, but nothing really made him feel as appreciated as it did to bake breads and cakes. He had even completed all his work for that day the night before meaning that he could work on anything that he wanted to.

He stretched as he got out of bed and opened the curtains to reveal a beautiful, sunny morning. He could not help but smile. Nothing could falter his mood today. Just a day of peace and quiet. He got dressed and made himself a morning coffee before going down into the ground floor of his bakery. He looked at his work top and imagined it to be fresh canvas waiting to be painted on by Picasso. He would make something outstanding today.

He was just about to decide on making a gingerbread house when there was an almighty clatter from above. He heard it before he saw what had happened. He threw himself to the floor upon the realisation that something had fallen through the top floor of his house and fell through to the ground floor. There was debris everywhere when he finally opened his eyes. He looked around speechless as it dawned upon him that his house and bakery was filled with dust and had been destroyed.

A small female creature lay in front of him. It had landed eventually on the work top that he been gazing upon. It looked as if she had fallen from some height. It didn't move for a while and he honestly believed it to be dead. With great strain, it eventually opened its eyes and groaned in pain.

"Vot is zis nonsense?" demanded the Baker in the most ridiculous accent that you could imagine whilst reading those four words. "I av spent hours ensuring zat zis place was spotless! All of a sudden zis teeny, little beast as destroyed my bakery!"

He looked outside further than the destruction of the bakery to the fresh countryside and harmonising day to try and calm himself. But it was impossible. Yet again they had done it. These stupid fairy tale creatures had ruined another perfectly good day. He grumbled with fury as he thought about it more. He hated all sorts of fairy take creatures and he hated where his bakery was located. He had tried to move his bakery away from all of them because he had once had an experience with a rogue gingerbread man. It had caused all sorts of madness and tarnished his reputation as a baker. It had finally met its end at the hands (or rather, in the mouth) of a fox. but the memories still haunted the Baker. He had lost all sorts of friendships because of its antics.

As for his bakery, well that was situated on one of the worst locations for anyone who hated those sorts of creatures. It sat at the bottom of a hill where a little boy and girl would frequently climb to fetch some water in a bucket. It was a large hill that was long in distance and covered with all sorts of those disgusting creatures.

First there was a cat who wore boots! BOOTS! One of the most ridiculous things that the Baker had ever seen. And the stupid cat was always always playing some happy go lucky song on a fiddle!

You wouldn't even want to get him started on the cow that just learned how to jump over the moon. Or how the cow would say moon. I'm pretty sure you can imagine how that would go! Cows shouldn't be jumping over moons. They should be in fields eating grass and providing milk for all good bakers.

Then there was the dog who laughed at seeing how silly they both looked. When have you ever seen a dog laughing? What a ridiculous thing. Dogs should not be laughing at cows. Dogs should especially noy be laughing at cats! They should be barking and chasing cats.

The icing on top of the cake was that there was a dish who had run away with a spoon. Although, nobody could ever tell you where to. Were they married now? Where did they run to? Are they running still?

The Baker wasn't going to take any more of this nonsense. Fairy tale creatures had it too good these days. There were rumours of a prison ship that dealt with them. Whatever the creature was that had destroyed his bakery. It was certainly due a visit to the ship.

CHAPTER FOURTEEN

The morning had not gone without it's problems. Mr Thomas was still ashamed to look Billy in the eye that morning even though Billy tried to tell him that he believed his pets were going to be okay. Mrs Thomas had come home from nightshift and had accidently drank some of Mr

Thomas's coffee believing it to be hot chocolate and was not lying in bed with her tired eyes wired open. Billy was quite happy to get out of the family home and make his way over to Mr Pets' Pet Store. He had ensured that he brought the book with him. Mr Pets was feeding a goldfish at the point when Billy had walked in.

"Don't need much food, do they? These little fellas," Billy stated. It sparked a conversation quite quickly with Mr Pets.

"You'd like to think that!" Mr Pets laughed. "People seem to think that they have very poor memories. Like when they say ""a memory like a goldfish."" Sometimes I like to think that if I sprinkle a little bit of food on this little fella's tank that he'll see it and go get some. Then while he's up there, forgets that I just did it a few seconds before and gets all happy again. And again. And again! Until he's eaten all his food. Strange, isn't it? How one of the smallest animals has apparently that sort of memory. Then an animal such as an elephant never forgets."

Perhaps because Mr Pets was talking nonsense anyway, it made Billy's conversation with him a great deal easier. He didn't really think that he needed to hold anything back and told him everything. He told him about how the Stog's had escaped their cage and the first had been placed into a book that contained a full spread story that now contained at least one of those characters. How the second had jumped out the window and was nowhere to be seen. But that the further and further that Billy ventured into the book, the more that the Stog's were mentioned.

Mr Pets was quiet for a little while. "I'm sorry son," were the first words that emerged from his mouth. "But without the physical species here I can't offer you a refund."

Kids, I know that I've mentioned this previously and this. ALMOST all the time your parents are right and that you shouldn't second guess them! But sometimes some **adults** can say the **stupidest things!** If you were ever to meet Mrs Barnett, I'm sure she'd be delighted in telling you some of the stupid things that the writer of this book has said or done (or even breathed).

Billy politely and calmly explained that that is not what he was looking for. He actually wanted to know if Mr Pet's had a copy of a book entitled *"The Stog's Wife"*.

"The Stog's Wife" was a book that used to read to him by his parents every night before he went to sleep when he was younger. He had unfortunately grown out of the book and had forgotten about those types of creatures that used to come around at night-time when children were asleep and cause havoc in their homes. However, when he looked through the story and saw the word "Stog" mentioned in the book he held in his hands he realised how stupid he had been. Those creatures that he had bought as pets weren't frogs of some sort of funny reptile; they were exactly how they were described in the picture books. It all came flushing back to him. Billy could remember a detail from the end of that book. Perhaps some of the children reading this or listening to it also remember that detail. By the end of that book, there was more than two Stogs!

If there was any way that the Stogs were going to get help in the story, it couldn't be done by any human. It would always have to be by fictional creature. Or in this case... Three unhatched Stog eggs!

CHAPTER FIFTEEN

They waited at the Dock. They were miles from anywhere. No creature ever travelled this far. Not a butcher, nor a candle stick maker, nor any fairy tale creature... Except a Baker! A Baker who had captured the Stog's Wife!

The sun was setting, the moon was beginning to rise from beneath the clouds in the sky. There had been a subtle change to the temperature. It had got really, really cold. Like if you were asleep and then you found that you started to shiver and you needed to grab yourself another blanket. Or a hot water bottle! You know, one of those really cold nights!

The Baker had taken control of the situation of the creature falling through the sky and through his bakery. He had trapped the creature into a jar and had summoned a prison ship that he knew of that would take care of the creature and he would never have to see or hear from it again.

The Stog's Wife was trapped within the small jar that the Baker used for jam. There wasn't much room for her in there to get up to mischief and it was easy for the Baker to carry. He was waiting for the HMS Jolly Roger to make port so that he could catch up with an old acquaintance. That acquaintance just happened to captain the prison ship for fairy tale creatures. Perhaps the Baker might even get a small token as a reward for bringing in a creature that no one had ever recorded before.

It was at least another hour after they had arrived before they started to see any sign or shape of any ships making port. But there it was! It soared through the ocean with immense pride, its sails gliding boastfully in the wind. It didn't take much longer after its initial sighting to bring itself into dock. It took almost another thirty minutes or so for the ship to secure itself into the dock.

This was the first time in a long time that anyone had seen the prison ship in all its glory. Its tall mast soared towards the sky and paraded jet black and golden lined sails. On its deck were sparkling clean floors that the crew must have been working on tirelessly. Its cannons sparked a purple reflection of the full moon. The bow of the ship had one of the most bizarrely decorated mermaid figureheads that had ever seen. It was as if the mermaid's hair was carved into the shape of tangled snakes. It had sharp teeth and raging eyes of fury.

The HMS Jolly Roger put almost every ship to shame as the Baker had watched it come in. If he had wanted a life on the sea, it would have been on this ship. Every second that it had taken to draw closer, the smile of the greedy Baker's face grew. Eventually you could see all his pearly white shine in the moon...

Ewwww!!! Hang on a minute! Those are not pearly white. That is a man who does not know how to brush his teeth properly! No, I'm being serious! Take a look:

No brushing!

No flossing!

No mouthwash!

Just yellow and missing teeth!

Once the ship had docked he watched as a figure from his school days disembarked and slowly made his way towards the Baker. Every step echoed against the wooden dock. It stopped and they stood in silence for a moment. Hook glared at the Baker. There was an undying hatred that would not diminish in his eyes.

Neither of them had really been friendly in the past but had spent time together in three of the same classes in high school. Hook had been a quieter student at the time and had started to take interest in the things those teenage boys do. He read a lot and spent a lot of time drawing and was interested in girls who were **waaaaayyyy** out of his social class. To cut it short, Hook was considered as an outcast even in his school years.

The Baker on the other hand had been a real sports player and had spent a lot of his years making a name for himself as a bit of a joker. A joker who loved nothing more than to pick on anyone who was not considered to be within his social class. When it came to Hook, the Baker had made it his mission to make his school time almost unbearable. Neither of them had spoken to each other or seen each other for years. This chance encounter seemed more that like they were both there to try and outdo the other in their accomplishments.

"Well well well," started the Baker. "James Hook."

"Clarence," Hook acknowledged almost disturbed to be breathing the same air as the man.

"Heard that you'd been awarded this," the Baker began with his small talk. Hook never really paid attention to the rest of what he said. Quite honestly, Hook would have preferred him just to say the truth:

"Never thought you'd be one to achieve anything like this. Took you some time though, didn't it? Was it true that you spent fifteen years captaining a bunch of pirates? Wow!

Yet here you are, just chasing a bunch of ridiculous creatures from other people's imaginations!"

"Well, we can't all be pastry sell outs. Can we?" Hook muttered under his breath

Hook had done his research on the Baker prior to making this little visit. The Baker had maybe just lost a little bakery he was operating but he had sold aa great deal of his company last year to a bakery branch that you may all be quite familiar with. They're very well known for their sausage rolls and steak bakes. He had a secret recipe that he had sold for millions. He'd literally become a millionaire overnight.

"You know, I don't really like pirates and boats. It's just silly role playing for adults," the Baker remarked. Overall he was unimpressed with what Hook had presented to him. "But when I heard it was you who that captained this ship - presumably still looking for a purpose - well I just had to come down and see it for myself. It's kind of nice having the options and free time. Just like it's good to know that some things never change."

Hook grabbed the jar from the Baker and walked away silently. He could feel the blood pumping furiously through his veins. The hairs stood to attention on the back of his neck because he was so angry. He should have never come here himself; he should have left it for one of the crew. After so long of being free from the anger; it had all tumbled back on top of him as if a wave from the sea. The Baker smirked and resorted back to the road. They never saw each other again but they're hatred of each other remained until the end of time.

The Stog's Stupendous Tale of Greatness will return after these messages:

In a world, divided by fear: one monster will do the unthinkable.... Have a great night out in the town. Filled with comedy, romance and adventure: Relive the sixties comedy classic in:

MR MONSTER GOES TO TOWN

THIS SUMMER!

Take another trip back to that wizard school you like so much! In a world divided by fear, one wizard boy will not be able to live up to the heritage that previous wizard's have. Nominated for seven "Worst Of" Categories enjoy the wizarding spectacular

Michael Flame : Boy Wizard

We now return to to the The Stog's Stupendous Tale of Greatness

CHAPTER SIXTEEN

"Who are you?" snarled Hook through the jam jar.

Even with the protective layer of glass, Hook was so close to the Stog's Wife that she could smell what he'd had for his dinner. Let me tell you something kids, the Stog's Wife could confirm to you - then and there - that codfish, garlic bread, onion gravy and chips fried in yesterday's oil does not make for a good smell!

He released her from the jar once they had returned to the Quarters. She was placed on the very chair that her husband had been sitting on previously. Although, she did not know that yet. She also didn't know that the man in front of her had been in a completely different mood when he had encountered the Stog. His meeting with the Baker must have put him in a foul mood because he was not being at all pleasant.

"I've been trying to work out what sort of story you come from. You and the other one. I own every fairy take ever written and don't have a clue what you are. My patience is trying!"

The Stog's Wife didn't answer any of his questions. She paid attention to the one sentence that he said that made her think there was hope after all. The ordeal with the Baker had put her in a foul mood. She was possibly even more angry than Hook was. All she wanted to do now was find her husband. She mustered the courage to finally speak.

"The other one?..."

Hook must have disliked how the Stog's Wife answered his question with a question. He sat down across from her (in the exact position he had when he was with the Stog) and placed his chin into his hand. His elbows leant upon the table and he placed his forefingers against the brim of his nose deep in thought about what he was going to do to her.

The only difference there was between the Stog originally meeting Warden Hook and the Stog's Wife now meeting him was that the table was now entirely covered with well-presented food. A plump roasted bird in the middle surrounded by all sorts of accompanying meats, vegetables and sauces. It was a dinner to die for that the cook had most likely spent most of the day working on. It could have been that Hook hadn't received the answer that he was looking for, or perhaps the mood that he was in because of the Baker, or even just because he was not a nice man. However, no one got to eat that dinner because Hook went into a blind rage and started to scream as he shot up from his chair and started throwing all the food, cutlery and dishes all over the room.

To change the perspective of this chapter slightly we're now going to look at this detail from the eyes of another individual. Every time that Hook's dinner was presented to him it was customary of his Head Chef to stand in the corner of the room and ensure that Hook was satisfied with his meal. Sometimes, he could be stood there for hours. It was part of the job that most chefs would have hated but Phileepe was a proud man and proud of the food that he made. He wanted to ensure that everything was perfect for the great Warden Hook. Now, when you've been working all day to ensure that your captain is happy with food it is disheartening to see that food thrown off the table and onto the floor. Hook didn't even have any dogs who would be able to eat the food off the floor. I can't say for certain that there were tears in Phileepe's eyes that evening but it would be a solid assumption.

Imagine graduating the top of your class at Chef School. Followed by being offered Head Chef at many of the top restaurants in France. Places such as

L'hôtel Vraiment Très Chic

Fantaisie et Swank

Hôtel de Posh

Dépensiers D'argent

Classe Supérieure

The top restaurants in France had all been begging and bargaining to bring Phileepe into head their teams. However, he turned his back on France and went to work on one of the most pristine ships ever built. Wouldn't you have thought that you had finally made it? But seeing all of your hard work just thrown to the floor like it was just a bunch of rubbish..... Three days in a row! These were the broken dreams of Phileepe and silently (but still proudly) he walked out of the door and back into the kitchen. If you listen very quietly, I think you can maybe still hear that poor man crying somewhere!

None of this made any difference to Hook or the Stog's Wife. To be honest, I don't think that they had noticed his existence. Hook cornered the Stog's Wife on top of her chair and then placed the tip of his hook underneath her chin. Its point digging in slightly as he growled through clenched teeth.

"I'm not going to ask again." He was sweating and his voice was shaking with fury. His eyes glared at her and they did not blink. She could see an untamed fire inside of them that burned like molten lava. His hair stood on end. "Tell me who you are or...." He tried to calm himself so that the threat seemed legitimate ".... Lucinda is going to get very thirsty."

Now I've seen grown men cry at threats such as this. Especially when it's a mad man pirate threatening them. Regardless of the new title that they have been given. Scenarios such as this can be the thing of nightmares. However, the Stog's Wife was not going to be intimidated by a bully and she did something did put Hook right into place.

She placed his hook down and shot her head forward quicker than a hound. She clenched her teeth so fast that she didn't even know she had done it and bit Hook right in the middle of his great big nose. The surprise and agony were too much for Hook. He howled like an injured dog until she let go. His howl must have been heard from some distance because the next thing that was heard was the response of wolves howling from miles and miles away.

"How dare you?" she began in a soft but stern voice. "I am a guest on your ship and this is how you treat your guests?"

Hook was flabbergasted at the response. No one had ever spoken to him like this and yet he was too afraid to answer back.

"Let me tell you something mister," she continued. "I do not care how much of a bad day you have had. Today I have been:

- Stuffed into two different containers that were supposed to be for snakes
- The first was supposed to contain a snake that was going to eat me!
- Then, I had the horrific experience of being thrown out of a window.
- Then falling from a great height and having the pleasure of meeting your vile Baker companion who – at first glance of me – stuffed me into a jam jar!
- And now am being threatened by a man who is so unaware of everything that he has got going from him got a little rattled by a comment made by his childhood bully.

I will not stand for it. Do you hear me? How dare you think of pushing people around like tha? You ought to be ashamed of yourself!"

Hook looked to the floor in shame for a moment. Was she right? Was this what had become of him. A petty little man looking for the approval of people from a life time ago?

"And one more thing," the Stog's wife continued. "You keep asking what on earth I am. I am a Stog. If there is one thing that Stog's know, it's that respect has to be earned and is not bought through fear or intimidation. I hope that you're proud of yourself."

She had taken it a step too far. If she had left it then perhaps Hook would have changed his ways. Perhaps he'd have decided that the life of a pirate (or even the sea) was not for him and gone into retirement. Imagine seeing Hook on a beach just relaxing with a rum and coke, watching the sun set each night, getting a tan and just chilling. That would have been a nice ending for the character.

In fact, we could have probably ended the book there and the Stog's could have gone back to their book and perhaps one day we would have all found out together what was going to happen with their children. Maybe *"Christmas Stoggings"* could have been something that we all looked forward to in the future because the story would have been open ended.

But that is not what happened! She had mentioned the name "Stog". Hook's eyes lit up like a candle being ignited. He now knew what they were. They weren't Fairy Tale creatures at all. They had fallen into his prison ship by nothing more than accident. Maybe he shouldn't just be dealing in fairy tale creatures after all. Heck, the prison ship was big enough. Maybe he should start going for all the creatures in every book. Then there would be no more need for reading. Or imagination. He could be the sole story that everyone could read.

"The Trials and Tribulations of Warden James Hook" written by Warden James Hook.

He liked the sound of that. Thunder started to roar outside of the ship and lightning began to strike the sea. The ship began to wave this way and that. A sinister smile on his face grew. He was no longer just the Warden of a Prison Ship. He would set out to become the only fairy tale that anyone would ever hear about.

He ordered his crew to deal with the Stog's Wife and left the quarters. With a sputtering and savage laugh that brought a newfound fear into the Stog's Wife.

CHAPTER SEVENTEEN

"Get back in there, you animal!" demanded the pirates with laughter and mockery.

Savagely they threw the Stog back into the cell he had been. They had thrown him in so hard that the uncontrollable speed stopped when he crashed into the wall at the back of the cell. It had been a little while since he had been in Hook's quarters. Ever since he had seen what Hook had let happen to the fairy, he had been mute. The pirates had taken him onto the poop deck for a while whilst they were heading to land and serenaded him with their strange made-up shanties and despicable tricks.

There had been songs that didn't make sense:

"Yo Ho! We'll sail through the sea!
A Pirates life for you but no, not for me!
Yo Ho! First mate Steve's sewing mittens!
Singing "" It's not good bye to you lads, it's simply good riddance!""

It wasn't the best lyrics that they had ever come up with. Unfortunately, it was one of those annoying songs that he where the lyrics stayed in his head, like an ear worm. Whilst it played on loop, his body lay motionless. He could not bring himself to stand up and comfort all the other creatures in their cells. They were aware of how bad Hook could be. But not very many of them could have known about the secret library. Or the book that diminished the existence of fairy tale creatures.

"Hey kid," whispered the Pig as the pirates left the cell block. "Kid, are you okay?"

He didn't answer. He didn't know if he should.

"The captain has beaten him," came a voice from across the cell block. Prisoner Pan was no longer whimpering like he had been the first time the Stog was in the cell block. The captain has broken his spirit. He's just like Pan."

"Shut it you!" the Pig bellowed towards Pan. He didn't say it but he was worried that Pan might be right.

The Stog turned away from them both and observed the darkness at the in the farthest corner of his cell. That's all he wanted to see. It almost seemed too miserable to be true. The Stog had never known dismay and deception or cruelty that Hook had shown. He'd never experienced anything like that in his own series of stories. Perhaps this adventure was a little too bit big for him. Afterall, he was just a tiny creature who caused mischief when children went to bed.

"Kid…" the pig started again. Before he could finish what he was going to say the corridor doors burst open again.

The two pirates who had taken the Stog out of his cell originally were back. Both laughing at all their prisoners misery the same way that they had been before. Strangley, they were not alone this time. They had another little prisoner with them. They stopped at the Stog's cell and opened it up again.

"Captain found you a little gift mate," grinned the first pirate as he threw in the second prisoner and locked the cell door again.

As they laughed and howled walking away, the Stog turned to see perhaps the most wonderful person that he could have ever wished to see. She was slightly messy and a little bruised but the Stog's Wife was as thrilled to see him as he was her. He jumped from the floor and ran into her arms. They embraced for some time. It could have been forever and it still wouldn't have been long enough.

The Pig beamed a smile that he didn't know he had left in him at the reunion of the two creatures. None of the prisoners ever saw any happiness in the cell block. Across the corridor in the opposite cell, Prisoner Pan had began bawling again. Although this time, it seemed to be more because he was happy for them.

"I was starting to think that I would never see you again," the Stog told his wife as they stopped hugging.

"Oh sweetheart," she replied. "If there was ever any creature to go on a most ridiculous adventure, it would most certainly be a Stog."

He smiled back at her. She was right. This had been what he had always wanted. He wasn't going to waste such an escapade feeling sorry for himself.

"The Warden has gone mad!" the Stog's Wife alerted as many of the prisoners as she could. "I don't know how he thinks that this prison ship is going to hold them all but he's going to find fictional characters and get rid of stories for all."

There was an outroar of alarm. The Pig tried to calm it down.

"That's not possible," the Pig assured them all. "He doesn't have anywhere to store that many fictional creatures!"

The Stog thought back to the library. How easy it was for Hook to dispose of the fairy. Hook wasn't talking about just imprisoning creatures. He was going to destroy them.

"I think that Warden Hook needs to remember who he is dealing with," the Stog announced. "He thinks that he has broken us. That putting us all in here will separate us from doing what each of us do best. But that's where he's wrong. He seems to forget that we have got in here, the one person that he was truly afraid of."

The Stog and the Pig looked over across the corridor. All of the prisoners in their cells started to look the same way. It was like they had all just realised that there greatest chance of beating Hook had been the one cell that they had all thought would have been the weakest.

"Why is everyone looking at us?" Prisoner Pan questioned.

CHAPTER EIGHTEEN

It was calm on the sea that evening. The HMS Jolly Roger sailed slowly in the middle of the ocean. The silence was broken by laughter and joyous songs sung by the pirates as they continued with their work and drank tankards of mead but below in the cell block contrasted completely from above.

The lanterns above were the only form of light and there had been hushed whispers for hours. Each of the creatures knew what they had to do. If they were going to escape, then their plan had to work like clockwork. Several of the characters were essential to the plan and would be the ones who would make their escape first and free the rest of the creatures.

It had just gone midnight when the pirates came down the same way that they always did to feed them. Portions of cold soup were passed into the cells by the cook and the two pirates that often walked the cell block. It was a little later for them than usual. They must have had a fair drinky poo before they came down because there were hiccups from all three of them as they started into yet another rendition of a song that no one had ever heard of. The song went a little bit like this

"Now laddies and lasses I can't hold a tune
But this wee sea shanty's a warning of doom
For you'll think that your safe on top of the land
All grassy and concrete on top of the sand.
But heed this grave warning or you'll find yourself dead
By a savage gold monster living under Peterhead"

"These songs get worse as they go on," the Stog whispered to his Wife. She chuckled slightly, keeping her volume down. The Stog looked over at the Pig and signalled him that the plan was to begin.

The Pig acknowledged the Stog and then slowly walked up to his cell bars. The pirates were still some distance away. He knew that if he was going to get their attention then he was going to have to be loud and obnoxious. He started groaning loudly and rattled himself against the cell bars.

"Hey!" he shouted so loudly that it echoed throughout the cell corridor multiple times. "Can you guys just SHUT UP!"

Obviously, statements such as this is going to attract some attention! Have you ever been that rude to your parents? Perhaps, perhaps not. Although I would highly not recommend being that rude to a bunch of pirates!

They were silenced by the sudden outburst of unpopularity and drew their attention away from the serving of cold soup. All three of the pirates left the boiling pot of soup and dragged themselves reluctantly towards the cell where the heckle had come from. They found themselves outside of the Pig's cell. There were some brief chuckles and grunts from the pirates but nothing that could be constructed clearly as words. He was being unusually brave and stubborn with his remarks this evening. Especially for someone who could easily be turned into bacon!

"Geez Louise! You guys are the worst singers that I have ever heard," the Pig spat at them with a gleeful smile on his face.

It was almost as if he enjoyed insulting the pirates. And after they had been SSSSOOOOOOO nice to him. You know, not turning him into pork and all!

"You know why is so rare that you hear about singing pirates?" The Pig questioned them.

For a brief second it seemed as if the pirates were genuinely at a loss for words. It was a fair question. Think about it, do you know of much singing pirates?

"Because nobody wants to hear a singing pirate," the Pig bellowed with laughter. "You're no good!"

Although the pirates looked speechless perhaps astounded at the vulgarity of the Pig's relentless interruptions, they all looked at each other in mutual agreement. The rum had clearly got to the pirates. Perhaps they had had a little too much whilst conducting their duties that evening. However, it worked out more for the Pig as they hiccupped uncontrollably and staggered as they attempted to place the cell key into the keyhole.

"You know – hiccup - what PIG? I've been waiting to do this for a long, long time!" muttered the first pirate only just able to understand.

He was swaying side to side. The ship wasn't even swaying that badly!

"Why should we just eat soup along with you disgusting creatures?" he continued. "When there are perfectly – hiccup - good sausages and pork right here?"

With that, they swung the door open swiftly. It slammed against the next cell and the metallic echo was sent through the whole corridor. The pirates were too focused on the Pig to notice that the Stog's Wife had been waiting for this opportunity. Carefully she grabbed the key through her own cell and after a little bit of fidgeting managed to pull it through.

As the pirates laughed maliciously, they cornered the Pig in his cell. He was starting to sweat. What a delicacy they had on their hands. This is what they should have always been doing. Rather than attempt to be nobleman, they should play their role as corrupted pirates with pride and without prejudice.

"Stop!" came a bellowing voice from behind them.

The pirates turned. Their eyes shot towards the door. They were surprised to see that the voice had come from the tiniest most insignificant creature that they had ever seen. He looked at them with a hard stare unblinking and never faltering. The Stog's cell was open and he stood outside the Pig's cell stubbornly. He remained silent and glared at them.

The pirates couldn't help but howl with laughter at even the faintest idea that this stupid, little creature was trying to protect the Pig. That laugh was the last that any of them would raise in the cell block. The last laugh that they would conjure on the ship. It was the final hurrah for the pirates. As they started to make their way from the Pig and towards the creature, immediately the Stog opened up his mouth and let out a giant burp realising a giant snake!

The snake paraded through the air in a wonderful glory. It's mouth wide open and starving, it devoured one of the pirates whole almost immediately before turning his eyes on the next. I can't put into words how momentous the occasion was in the cell block, the closest thing towards it that I can provide is this picture! Look at it! Look at the majestic moment:

Excuse you? What do you mean that the snake was a conveniently placed plot point at the start of the book?

*I'll have you know that I never said that the Stog chewed him up! Infact, if you refer back to that chapter (and I bet you will!) I think that you'll find that the exact words that I used were "as such the terrifying snake isn't so terrifying because he's now been **swallowed whole!**" Could you even imagine chewing a snake? It would be all slimy and scaly. What do you think I am? Some sort of monster? I can guarantee you that no animals were harmed in the making of this story!*

Back to it!...

The cell block occupants cheered and rallied around their cells. It was the most outrageous display that any of them had seen ever since they had been brought aboard the ship. The Pig belched and bellowed with laughter at the sight of two other pirates frantically weeping and running from a hungry snake. They clambered above cells and begged it to stop as the Stog, his wife and the Pig ventured towards the cells and freed the occupants from them. It was the first time that many of them had smiled in a long time. Seeing pirates terrified and nothing more than the frightened men that they had proven themselves to be brought a sense of power towards them. Why were they afraid of these men? Why had it been so long that they had had to put up with the nonsense that the pirates had served them.

The Stog and his wife led the crew of escapees to the cell block. The screams and whimpers of the pirates echoed through the hall. Before they could even break out, other pirates started coming from all directions wondering what all the noise was about. They were so distracted with a large snake that had got a taste for pirates that they had not noticed that every single jail cell was empty. As quietly as they could, the escapees made their way out of the cell and towards the Captain's quarters above deck.

CHAPTER NINETEEN

There could have been another chapter dedicated towards the creatures secretly making their way towards the quarters. However, you as the reader should know that every single other pirate that wasn't pre-occupied with the snake incident were nowhere to be seen. It was the quietest part of the story. I couldn't have made it exciting even if I wanted to!

The Captain's quarters were unlocked and there was not a single person in there either. Even getting the mirror to open was one of the easiest things that they had endured! Whilst the Stog , his wife, Prisoner Pan began to look for books that would be useful in aiding them to escape, the Pig was being helped by the puppet with the nose problem began to collate anything that they could to block the entrance behind the mirror.

There wasn't a single book title that was remotely helpful. For such a collector of books that were drawn behind chains and almost impossible to unbind, the books were possible some of the most boring titles that could not (and more probably would not) be read by children. The book titles ranged from

The Pythagoras Theorem that doesn't include Pie!
Vincent Van Gogh's Secret Vincent Van Gone Lifestyle
How To Brew Your Own Coffee
How To Grow Your Own Coffee Beans
How To Give Up On Your Original Idea and Make Tea Instead
Pirates Life: Is It Really the Life For You?
Dear Diary: A Beginner's Guide
How To Play Guitar In Six Easy Steps
How To Play Guitar In An Even Easier Twelve Steps
So You're Not Very Good At Guitar and You Need to Lean In Eighteen Steps
Here's How You Hold A Guitar, You Knit Wit!
Eggs!!!

It was no use! It didn't seem like there was anything that would be any help!

"What are we going to do?" Pan started to panic. "If the Captain finds us then he will hurt us again. I can't go through all of that again."

The Stog continued to search frantically. He was looking for anything that might be able to help them. The Stog's Wife stopped upon hearing Pan's worrying. She went over to comfort him so that his worrying would not give away their position.

But it was too late!

They could hear rumblings start to move outside of the blockade. Pan's worrying started to get a worse and eventually he was being so loud that it would have been impossible for them to remain hidden for any longer. The noise from outside had turned into mocking laughter and threatening words. The blockade wouldn't hold for long. The fairy tale creatures pulled away from it, all conducting the same frantic searching through books that the Stog was.

It was no use. The blockade held no longer. It didn't take very long for the library to be filled with blood thirsty pirates. There were laughs and growls like untamed bears as the Stog and his wife looked around in terror. The pirates pushed the Stog, his wife and the other creatures together in the centre of the room and they were trapped. Everywhere that they looked was another pirate that was more dreadful and unclean than the last.

They were drawing in closer and closer. It didn't look like they had much of a chance anymore. They all wracked their brains to think of something – anything – that might be their last hope. The library was becoming too cramped. There was no room for any of them to move. There was no hope.

"You better stop this right now and go to your room!"

The pirates stopped exactly where they were. They looked at the Stog with a little bit of confusion. He looked back at them possibly even more confused at what had just happened. They all looked towards his wife (who had made the command) and then to each other to make sure that each of them had heard the same thing.

"I am not impressed with any of you! We are trying to get back to our children and you have all been nothing but a nuisance! If you want to act like children, then you can go to your room like children," the Stog's Wife demanded again. She was wearing the same look that she had when she had given Hook into trouble before for being rude.

The pirates still stood frozen in utter disbelief. The Stog could see that they did not know what to do. He held tightly onto his wife's hand. She clenched his and he got a warmth of courage that he had not felt since they had entered this strange new world.

"We mean it!" he began in a stern voice, "I am deadly serious! I am very, very angry with all of you. I am very very annoyed. You should all get out of my sight before I contact each and everyone of your parents..."

This time the pirates looked slightly flustered and worried at the thought that their parents could be called. Yes kids, even pirates know that they have gone too far if their mothers and fathers are about to be called.

The Stog and his wife looked at each other, they were very much aware that pirates were not used to being talked to in such a way. They just had to play their cards right and hopefully the pirates would succumb to their demands.

"Go... To ... Your... ROOM!" the Stog growled at them all. It was in a voice that even surprised himself. It sounded angry and disappointed all at once. Like a father that was disciplining his own children for misbehaving.

Slowly – but most definitely surely – there were shuffles backwards. The pirates no longer looked proud or scary. Some started to hang their heads in despair and worry. Miraculously, it seemed to be working. The Stog's Wife let out a little sigh of relief as they continued to walk back. Each pirate whimpering as if they knew their parents would be deeply disappointed in them. The fairy tale creatures from behind the Stog and his Wife also began to get a little more confident as well as they watched the pirates walk away in dismay.

A voice carried over from the crowds. It was recogniseable in an instant. It shot up the fairy tale creatures like a sting from the coldest of ice. It was as if they went stiff from fear. "Are you kidding?" it questioned the crowd. "Lads, are we not pirates?"

"Errr ... aye?" came a different voice from the crowd. It almost sounded like it needs convincing. There were a few murmurs in the crowd that mirrored the answer that it had given.

The original voice made its way to the front of the crew. The Stog's heart sank and his insides tightened up when he realised that it was Hook.

Not content with the response from his men, Hook stated "I'll ask again! Are we not pirates?"

The response that came from the crowd of pirates the second time needed very little convincing. They had spent some time trying to fit in with the world and taking their eyes off of the one thing that made them whole and made their lives worth living. Piracy. Why go along with the need to hold up fairy tale creatures and get paid like respectable men when they could do the one thing that they enjoyed. Dig for treasure. Steal ships and – most of all – drink rum!

"Aye!" Hook declared gleefully. Putting an end towards the charade that he could have been a better and respectable man. "And what do pirates not care about lads?" he questioned in a booming voice that neither the Stog or his Wife had ever heard him speak in since their arrival upon the ship.

There were a number of voices with suggestions. They were all shouting over each other to try and get the correct one. I wont lie to you either, pirates are not the most intelligent of people when it comes to very simple questions. Here's some of the more outrageousanswers that they gave:

"Unicorns?"

"The meaning of life?"

"Maths?"

"Sunsets?"

"The dichotomy of good and evil?"

I could go on with these answers, but I guess you get the drift!

"Repercussions?" came a voice from the back. It – like many of the answers before it - was more of a question. Out of all the answers that had been given, that was the one that Hook pointed out from the rest of them.

"Aye," Hook answered sinisterly. He turned from the crew and the looked towards the fairy tale creatures in the middle of the room. The remaining members of the crew turned back around to the creatures as well and circled around them again.

"Repercussions!" they chanted together whilst engulfing the space within the library again.

There was no way out. Nothing that any of them could do any more. They had to accept that this was that their attempt at escape had failed and every single one of them were to return to their cells and – most likely – face whatever vile punishment that Hook thought up for them.

That's how we'll end the chapter! It could be the end for them all. Although, I doubt that none were more disheartened than the Stog. I mean, his last words may have been to tell a crew of savage pirates to go to their bedrooms!

CHAPTER TWENTY

"Get them," demanded Hook. There was an aggression and power in his voice that the likes of had never been heard before, not even by his own men.

The room was full of carnage! It became like a series of tangled knots as the fairy tale creatures fought uselessly to try and break free from their captors. Throughout random parts of the library were the screams and whimpers of creatures that were captured by the pirates. Each time that a pirate caught one of them there were a round of cheers and merciless laughter. The noise could be heard all over the ship, without a doubt!

First, they grabbed the puppet boy. They started pulling him at both sides from his arms and his legs. He howled as they attempted to break parts of him off for firewood. The Pig squealed in an ungodly tone of fear of becoming tomorrow's breakfast. It echoed all throughout the room. Prisoner Pan whimpered as he crawled into a tight spot behind some of the stacks of books on the shelves. The pirates couldn't get to him but that didn't stop them laughing harrowingly and spitting at him like he was nothing.

Hook ignored all of them. His eyes – full of fire and rage – were focussed relentlessly upon the Stog and his Wife. How dare they? They were not even real fairy tale creatures! How dare they come upon this ship that he had built a reputation on as the finest of its kind and attempt to destroy its credibility. His reputation reduced to nothing more than a pirate. The disgusting smile on his face did not falter. He had plans for them. Plans that were reduced only to the worst of prisoners on his ship. The ones who could not fulfil their purpose and the ones – like the Stogs – who just would not get with the programme!

Hook's eyes changed direction swiftly for a second towards the books and the faur of the Stog's body stuck on end. A horrid, look of delight came upon Hook's face as he headed towards the book shelf. The Stog recognised the book he was looking at within an instant. Hook's good hand went towards the hundreds of books and he pulled out the one that the Stog recognised as the one that he had used to dispose of the fairy. Hook pointed it at the Stog's. They had no chance of escape in the chaos.

The book began to open. Colour began to drain the room. Everything felt cold. Happiness and warmth felt like they were nothing more than fiction. Hook's eyes widened with delight. The Stog and his Wife could feel themselves being pulled away from the world. Particles no bigger than dust starting to pull away from them and towards the book. A menacing laughter could be heard that echoed throughout the library. Every pirate and fairy take creature stopped and watched in shock and terror as it seemed as though the Stog's would be erased forever.

When suddenly, a small little rag doll fell onto the floor!

CHAPTER TWENTY-ONE

Hook closed the book. It was the most curious thing that he had ever seen happen on his ship. From out of no where this tiny battered little rag doll lay on the floor. It looked old and hideous. With great big eyes and untidy hair. It was one of the strangest things that he had ever seen.

"What's all this then?" he bellowed attempting to get his crew to join in with his mocking again. "A final attempt to bribe for your lives. Huh, this silly little doll?"

Then he noticed upon how the Stogs were also looking at the doll. They were struggling to catch their breath after their encounter with the book but it was very clear that they had never seen it before in their lives.

The rag doll looked ripped and tattered and didn't have much clothing. It was disgusting looking and almost frightening. Suddenly, thunder roared around them and lightning flashed the sea. From the darkest corners of the library came a monstrous voice that started to shake the whole room, perhaps even the whole ship. Deep and powerful, it was chilling from the moment it spoke. It recited words to a poem that none of them had heard before:

"The sun has set and the moon shines bright
On the start of this Halloween night
The "Guisers" of the "Trick of Treaters" start to sing
*The hallowed tale of **"Samantha on the swing!"""***

The crew were quicker to react than Hook was at the sound of the voice. Many enquired whether it was coming from the books. But that was ridiculous. Books didn't talk! Did they?

Hook remained suspicious that this was some trick that the Stog and his friends were playing on them as an attempt to escape. The Pig and the Puppet were the first to put these suspicions to rest with the way that they reacted. (The puppet announced, "I solemnly swear that I haven't a clue what is going on!". The Pig confirmed that his nose had not grown a millimetre.) The voice continued:

"Samantha is a patched-up doll
Samantha says nothing at all
Samantha's smile never seems to fall.
As she sits, Samantha on the swing!"

Although it seemed impossible, the doll quickly became more sinister looking. The lighting in the room started to dim. Through the tiny pentagon shaped windows some of the pirates began to remark on the growing clouds that darkened the skies. Thunder began to roar.

A pirate or two started to stare into the doll's eyes and realised that the words of the poem were not lying. The dolls eyes obviously didn't blink (as they were a rag dolls eyes!). But it's smile was sinister. Never faltering. Becoming more and more distasteful to look at as time went on.

It raised slightly, as though ghostly. The crowd around it were left dumb struck and in awe as it started swinging to and thro. Underneath her was a swing that no one had noticed. As their eyes adjusted to the darkness invoking the library, they could also make out chains that held the swing somewhere in the roof. Things were getting stranger as the voice continued.

"The wolves, they howl at the midnight sky
It's a doll they're scared of, yet they cry
Their howls scream out "why oh why?"
As she sits, Samantha on the swing!"

Rain started to smash against the windows. The wind howled loudly and unkindly. Between its screech and the growls of the thunder, howls could be heard in the distance. Some of the pirates mumbled incoherently but made very clear that they were no longer interested in the line of work that they found themselves in. They had always been told that sailing with Hook would leave them nothing but dismay. It almost looked that way.

Hook was unimpressed with the activities that surrounded him. Whether or not it was the work of the Stog and the fairy tale creatures he was losing the reassurance of his crew and the last thing that anyone needed at this moment in time was a mutiny.

"Cut your nonsense out, ye yellow bellied land lubbers!", he growled at them all. "Or it'll be the plank for ye!"

Undeterred the voice continued:

"Witches cackle and how they laugh
Mixing spells and potions inside of baths
Such a better way to do witchcraft
As she sits, Samantha on the swing"

There were cackles in the room as yellow blue and red remnants of smoke started to enclose them. Haunting laughter surrounded them. Cackles enveloped the laughter. If this was a trick it was a diabolical trick. No one had ever seen anything like this on the Jolly Roger before and it was becoming far too much for some of the pirates.

"Mummy's moan and zombie's groan
In creepy and exhausted tones
Past the trees they roam and roam
As she sits, Samantha on the Swing"

From all around them on different shelves of the library, some of the books started to fall.

"Curse of the Mummy" was a title of one.

Another being *"War of the Living Dead."*

The leather-bound books flickered open slowly; never settling on a page. Groans of pain, sorrow and morbid misery coming out of them. Everything thus far was happening all together. The crew were spooked. Even Hook started to look uncomfortable with everything that was going on.

Suddenly everything stopped. An unsettling silence encased the library. The pirates were speechless and the Stog's could not help but wonder what on earth was going to happen next? As if on cue, the voice exploded again reciting as if it had never stopped.

"Night turns silent
The night turns cold
Campers tell ghost stories old
She listens, Samantha on the swing

You hear the cawing of the crows
Feel worms wiggle between your toes
That's just how the story goes
She still sits, Samantha on the swing"

If they hadn't seen it with their own eyes, then they never would have believed it. The Stog's eyes fixed on the doll's face when it horrifically began to turn its head. It stayed in its upwards position before slowly turning its head towards theirs. Its mouth looked as if it was trying to move but then they realised that something was trying to escape from it.

The Stog's Wife held him tighter than ever. The Stog began to take steps away from the doll. However, his wife was frozen with fear. Whatever this doll was; it was even more terrifying than the anything that they had encountered throughout this whole escapade. All that they wanted was for it to end. But the voice continued:

"Samantha steals the eyes of frogs
She also steals the tails off dogs
She tries the eat the heads of Stogs
Although she sits, Samantha on the swing"

It was like a horror movie when the stitches began to release from the doll's mouth. From inside of it they saw a truly disturbing sight. A head of a fellow Stog! It was screaming harrowingly knowing that there was never an escape for it. The Stog and his Wife could do nothing. Their mouths dry and speechless. Their feet unable to move. The colour draining from their face. The doll was the worst thing that they had ever seen. The more that the voice recited the final verse of it's poem the more disgusted and scared that they were of the creature that dangled on a swing before them.

"Her hair gets chewed out by rats
Her stuffing scratched by black cats
She wants to fly like vampire bats
And she's up, Samantha on the swing!"

The doll jumped from the swing and landed on its two battered and torn feet. Unable to walk properly it limped forward slowly. Its balance was poor but it adjusted every so often as it improperly made its way towards anyone that would have contact with it.

The pirates had had enough. No job was worth the fear that the doll had put into them. They fled the library like wild rabbits, jumping over and pushing each other to try and get out of the quarter doors and towards the ship's lifeboats as fast as they could. Many of them no longer spoke words; simply stuttering gibberish as they tried to escape from the ship.

"Cowards! Cowards, the lot of ye! Get back here!" screamed Hook after his crew. But it was no use. The crew were gone. He was alone. Defenceless and at the mercy of the fairy tale creatures he had kept captive.

Steadily, the library began to light up. It looked almost exactly as it had done on the Stog's first encounter with it. The Stog and his wife slowly made their way to the doll that had fallen on the floor. It lay motionless for a moment or two. Their hearts skipped a beat as the padding at the back of it began to shuffle slightly. It was as if something was struggling to get out. It moved and sounded like a trapped mouse. The Stog overcame his cautiousness and was about to stamp on the moving creature.

He didn't need to. From underneath the rag doll's clothing came the happy smile of a baby Stog!

Tears of joy swelled within the Stog's wife eyes. She was speechless but ran towards the baby Stog, whisking it up from under the rag doll clothing and embracing it tightly. It was the happiest moment of her life. The Stog struggled to speak himself but had an overbearing warmth run through him that he had rarely felt before. It was a feeling of love and pride. They had finally been able to meet one of their children.

"What the heck is that over there?" questioned the Pig from behind them pointing towards the upper shelves from the library.

From high above, books started falling gracefully from the upper levels. They fell gracefully to start. Although, the more that kept falling, the harsher that they fell to the ground. something was pushing them down from behind as it made its way from the top of the bookcase towards the bottom. Once it reached the bottom, the shape was identified as another baby Stog although this one was bigger than the last, it was also a lot fatter and had the tiniest eyes that could be seen on any of the Stogs. He looked like a lizard or a frog. Finally, from behind the book shelf came the scruffiest looking Stog of the three children. It held a paper cone that could be used to magnify his voice. It appeared that all three of the baby Stogs had been able to get into the Billy's book!

It was honestly at that point that the Stog and has Wife believed that Billy and Mr Pets must have found the copy of *"The Stog's Wife"* that they had been looking for and used it to get the baby Stogs into the story. They had no way of knowing that the baby stog eggs were simply not there once they had found a copy (or in this case five copies) of the book. However, once the baby stogs had been able to get aboard Hook's prison ship they had concocted a plan in order to ensure that the pirates left.

"My babies!" the Stogs Wife cried her joyful tears. "I'm so happy to finally meet you all." She paused for a moment as she gave them all a giant hug. Her heart was full of warmth and the smile that was on her face seemed like it would never fade. Her children hugged her back as they had instantly identified her as their mother.

The Stog beamed behind them all with pride but was a little nervous of meeting his children for the first time. He knew that it was his fault that they were all here and not safely in their own story. He had out them all in danger. As he saw them all embracing for the first time, he felt an enormous amount of pride but also a little sick with shame. This should have been good enough for him from the start and it was only now that he was beginning to realise that. What did that mean? Was he good enough to be a father for the stog children?

Perhaps she sensed his worry and that in the moment he was not as confident as he could have been. But the Stog's Wife pulled away from her children with loving care and took a step back. With a gentle nudge towards her husband and a reassuring smile, she spoke softly to her children.

"Kids, I'd like you to meet your father. He's silly, ridiculous and sometimes he's just downright stupid. But I love him and I know that you're all going to love him too."

There was an awkward silence for a moment. The baby stogs looked their father up and down. Perhaps their minds could not comprehend that this was all that they were going to be given as a creature that was to protect them from harm and love them unconditionally. Then like a giant wave crashing across a sunset beach they ran towards him – just as they had done to their mother – and gave him a giant hug. His heart melted in that moment. It was as if all the worrying and fear went away. He knew that they loved him and he loved them.

So without keeping you in suspense any longer readers, I think that it's finally time for you to meet the new additions to the Stog family. You have two baby boys and a baby girl. Their names are Alice, Newt and Scruffball. Here's a picture of what they look like! Arent they cute?

No ... haven't you learned after all this story that you cannot keep a stog of any size as a pet! They just get into too much mischief!

The library gave a resounding cheer. Everyone was delighted at the arrival of the baby stogs. It should have been the most joyous of occasions. These types of moments would usually be the happily ever after of which a story end. As the writer, I wish that I could deliver that moment to you here. But I can't.

For you see, there's still a loose end or two that needs to be dealt with before we can finish this story. The pirates had fled the ship but in the middle of the room

surrounded by some begrudging fairy tale creatures stood
Warden Hook.

CHAPTER TWENTY-TWO

"The ship is ours!" cheered the pig.

The library erupted into an explosion of cheers. From
all corners and crevices, tens of hundreds of fairy tale
creatures (that are just far too many to list) started entering
the quarters and the library from all over the ship. If you look
at any of your books on any given bookshelf, the likelihood is
that there were some characters from those stories had been
set free from their cells. They were celebrating that they
could now run the ship as their own.

"No!" came a singular voice from one of the smallest
creatures aboard it. "The ship is his!"

There were murmurs as the crowd had gathered.
Some seemed to disapprove of the decision that had been
declared. Almost all of them looked around to find out what
sort of creature had made such an outrageous proposal. The
Stog stood at the centre of the library with his family by his
side. He too was looking around to see who would have
stated such a thing.

The voice was coming from above. It belonged to a
fairy that had been captive in a lantern like the one that the
Stog had previously encountered. It had a booming voice

very unlike the one that Hook had disposed of. But as it spoke every other creature remained silent.

"We must ensure," the fairy continued to his audience, "that nothing like this ever happens again! We must! Not for us. But for the many creatures that have remained free and were never prisoners of the HMS Jolly Roger! They must know that nothing like this will ever happen again!"

There were murmurs in the crowd again. Although this time they were a little quieter than they had been the first time around. Some of them were agreeing with the fairy. They had all been through a terrible time. To let the ship be captained by hundreds of fairy tale creatures that had been done wrong would not only end fairy tales as children knew them but could also teach future generations incorrect lessons.

"What do you suggest?" asked the Pig. He was the first voice of disapproval from the crowd that was brave enough to come forward.

Everyone stood in silence. He fairy had no answer to the Pig's question. No one could accurately tell you how long that they stood there delving the conundrum.

Finally, a voice spoke that no one expected to, or rather three:

"This ship belongs to the pirates. So let it just be that. A pirate ship!" Alice spoke. She was a little nervous in such a large group but everything that she said seemed to make sense.

"We've all got our own stories that we can get back to," Newt followed his sister slightly more confidently. "Let them get back to theirs."

"I just want to go home," finally said Scruffball. His voice was a little quieter and squeakier than his siblings, but the point stood well with the crowd.

The crowd nodded their heads in agreement. Holding a grudge and sailing the seas for revenge wasn't something that they wanted to spend the rest of their years doing. They wanted to spend their days capturing the imaginations of children and adults alike. Sharing the opportunities to have bedtime stories or hearing grown-ups use their voices to project stories to their offspring like they had done for years before.

The Stog and his Wife could not have been prouder of their children. Together with the rest of the creatures they started to collect the books from the library in search of their own stories so that they could all go home. Well, all the fairy tale creatures except one.

CHAPTER TWENTY-THREE

Depending on who you ask; there are two very different sayings when it comes to revenge being served.

For example, if you were to watch a ninety-minute action film - in which the lead character's loved ones were kidnapped and taken from them - the lead character would exact his revenge on the main villain within a short amount of time. In this context, the saying would be *"revenge is a dish best served hot."*

To contradict, if the same ninety-minute film flashed forward several weeks (or months, years or decades etc) then it may take the main character up to a lifetime to get revenge on the film's antagonist. In this scenario, the saying would be read as *"revenge is a dish best served cold."*

As a writer that has never served any dishes of revenge (being that either hot or cold) I couldn't possibly comment. However- as an observer of the characters in this story – I can tell you that this was not an option to Prisoner Pan.

If we look at the facts, we can indeed see why this scenario would be a prominent point of one of the closing chapters of this story. Prisoner Pan – or how some of you may have known him previously from a different story "Peter" – was a renowned hero in the fairy tale community. In that moment on the HMS Jolly Roger of forgiving (and even perhaps, forgetting) his rage overcame him.

Upon capture and becoming the first prisoner upon the HMS Jolly Roger, Prisoner Pan was subjected to many cruel, mundane and adult like tortures. Some of these included:

- *Working in a job that he was neither good at nor did he enjoy*
- *Trying to make ends meet on a low income*
- *Subjected to long and tedious lectures by a monotoned lecturer*

After a while, Prisoner Pan lost his childlike innocence and started seeing the world through the eyes of an adult. With his innocence went his hairline and youthful looks. A beer belly was added into his life whilst his childlike imagination and ability to fly were stolen from him. Eventually his mind was lost to the wasted 9 to 5 hours, endless calculations of money and the drones of lecturing. After enduring all of that, he was thrown into a prison cell and forgotten about. Time had not been kind to Prisoner Pan. He had sworn revenge on Warden Hook. In this case, revenge was going to be a dish that was most certainly better served ice cold.

"It doesn't happens!" spat Prisoner Pan shaking uncontrollably. Even the mere proposal of letting Hook go was enough to enrage him.

Pan emerged from the shadows. His receding hairline drenched in sweat and his eyes full of hate. He grabbed an abandoned sword that one of the fleeing pirates had left behind and pointed it towards Hook. He hissed and spat as he pointed the word. He was foaming at the mouth. His breaths were shrill and heavy. His eyes were blood shot and hadn't blinked for some time. He acted as if he was a starving animal. Furiously, he stormed passed The Stog's family and growled towards Hook.

Wind shrieked at a tone that was almost unheard of. Thunder roared ferociously as Prisoner Pan directed Hook out of the library. Hook tried to protest and pleaded with Prisoner Pan. However, all that gained was the attention of the other fairy tale creatures. A desiring fire began to burn in their eyes as they watched. They became intrigued that the one prisoner – that many of them had considered the weakest and most pathetic – was finally taking Warden Hook's destiny into his own hands. Lightning flashed forks of destruction in the darkness as Prisoner Pan ordered Hook outside towards the poop deck. Rain smashed against the ground as the untamed waves threw themselves over each other. The fairy tale creatures began to follow Pan out. Voices began to mumble and escalate behind him, encouraging him further in his motives.

In the commotion, the Stog tried to see what was going on. The crowd kept him from getting ahead of them but through them he could barely make out that Prisoner Pan was directing Hook towards the walking plank.

"What are you doing?" The Stog shouted desperately after him.

"He laughed at us!" screeched Pan not even looking back at the Stog. His eyes remained solely on Hook.

Prisoner Pan knew that Hook had taken everything away from him that he had once known. Not just his friends, his innocence and sense of wonder ... but - most of all - his own story. He had been a beacon of hope for the adventurous and (to a certain degree) the immature. All he had was now the memories of such a time. As fleeting series of moments in a much depressingly aging body.

"He humiliates us! Tortures us!" he screeched again. He never lowered his sword or his gaze. "We waited and waited! We'll never be free! Stuck as this! Always this! ... He walks! He walks!!!"

Prisoner Pan continued directing Hook towards the walking plank at the side of the ship. Hook could see the venomous disgust that surrounded him from – not only Prisoner Pan – all of the fairy tale creatures. As he got closer to the plank above the untamed sea, his lips began to curl into a sinister smile.

The fairy tale creatures started to chant. "PLANK! PLANK! PLANK!" They were unified in their hate for him. Not even one of them were trying to aide him. The delicious smile curled even more around his lips as he began to encourage them to throw him from the plank themselves. Not a single one of them was attempting to help him. As he was surrounded by the fairy tale creatures – with no where to go but the plank – he couldn't help but be incredibly impressed that they were now like pirates and their innocence (much like Prisoner Pan's) had disappeared. He had won. They weren't fairy tale creatures anymore. They were repressed individuals that were bringing anarchy where ever they would roam.

The Stog and his family struggled and squeezed as they attempted to make their way towards Pan and Hook. They were disheartened to see the Pig and the Puppet Boy as part of the crowds. They were both chanting along with the rest of the crowd. They had made their decision as well from the moment that Pan had picked up the sword. Even the Pig and the Puppet boy turned their backs on the Stog.

"Walk!" ordered Pan as Hook stumbled upon the blank. The sea staggered and moaned underneath them. "WALK!" he screamed again

The resounding chant changed Prisoner Pan furthered his victim towards his demise. *"Walk, Walk Walk!"* There was nothing that anyone could do. *"Walk, Walk Walk!"* It looked like the end of fairy tale creatures as we knew them. *"Walk, Walk Walk!"* Nothing more than a dismay of creatures' blood thirsty for revenge. *"Walk, Walk Walk!"* Not a decent soul inside any one of them. *"Walk, Walk Walk!"*

Before we end this chapter, I would like you as the reader to remember that there is always hope. For this chapter will be end on a happier note due to one of the most remarkable things that any child has... Their imagination!

If you remember early on, I told you that Billy Thomas was a child who was brave, kind and selfless. He knew that he had altered the lives of all the Stog family when he had purchased them from Mr Pets Store. He also knew that it was not for the better, they were way in over their heads in a story that did not belong to them.

The act of a child that is kind and selfless can be anything. Which is even more fascinating when the act can come from an unfiltered imagination. In this case – through the horrific gales, roars of thunder and torrential lightning - a single piece of paper danced through the wind and landed into the Stog's hands through all the commotion. His eyes widened with delight and yearning as he read it aloud:

"Dear Stog Family,

My name is Billy Thomas. I am the boy that bought you and your wife from Mr Pet's Pet Store.

I am terribly sorry that I have got you into all this mess. Mr Pets and I have been reading all about your adventures on the HMS Jolly Roger. This was a story that my father wrote but never finished. We decided to end it in a special way to help you and all the other fairy tale creatures.

I may grant you one wish. It can be anything. All you must do is close your eyes and wish for whatever you want.

I hope that this makes amends for some of the ordeals that you have been through

Billy Thomas, Aged 9"

"My goodness," declared the Stog's Wife after hearing the letter read aloud. "How kind and helpful!"

She was not the only one that had heard. The letter had got the attention of the fairy tale creatures who had drawn their attention from Warden Hook. Prisoner Pan was the only one still with his eyes on him.

"What do we wish for?" the Pig shouted.

"It should be my wish!" The Puppet Boy screeched. "I have suffered the most throughout this whole escapade." (His nose grew at that point).

The commotion started to get louder. The Stog and his family were now surrounded by the crowd. They were unable to concentrate. They couldn't decide what to wish for. The shouting and arguing of the fairy tale creatures all becoming too much for them to cope with. Then it was broken by one resounding scream.

"No!!!" came the undeniably shrilled scream of Prisoner Pan. "What's it doing?"
The Stog family's eyes shot towards Prisoner Pan faster than a shooting star. The fairy tale creatures were a little slower. All of them were looked towards the plank that Prisoner Pan was pressuring Hook to walk upon. Prisoner Pan was screaming uncontrollably towards Warden Hook. It

didn't even sound like words but a series of jumbled up letters. He couldn't formulate words upon staring at Hook's actions.

Hook stood at the end of the plank with his eyes closed in undisturbed zen. When he opened them his eyes showed remorse for the first time throughout Prisoner Pan's whole experience. Without warning, he took one final step off the plank and fell towards the ocean without a sound. The fairy tale creatures and Prisoner Pan all stood in shock and awe as a blinding light overtook the scene. Of all the unredeemable characters that could have achieved any victory upon the HMS Jolly Roger; Warden Hook had made a wish that would never been known by any of them until it had fully formed. The Stog and his family held together. Some of the fairy tale creatures shielded their eyes from the blinding white light that eclipsed over them. The only sound that could be heard was Prisoner Pan's final dismal screeches of unrealised revenge. The light finally overcame them all and settled into the quiet, blankness of the next page...

CHAPTER TWENTY - FOUR

The classroom was boring. That's the only way to describe it!

You know your classroom that you have at school? The one that is possibly filled with colourful posters of the subjects that you are learning and a big black board that the teacher uses to teach you? The one you may have to go back in tomorrow and tell your teacher of yet another great chapter in this great story! Well, the classroom that Billy usually attended with those three other students that we mentioned at the start of the book *(and I promised would come back at some point)* didn't have that sort of atmosphere. There was nothing in it except four tables (one for each student), a grey wall with no posters or decorations (there was one plain white clock so that they could tell the time) and a few dusty books that were just stacked upon each other in the corner. There wasn't even a teacher!

Well, Grr Lee, Princess and Summer were all sat in there the day after the Stog family had been sucked into Billy's book. Billy also would usually attend school every day but because we know that he was trying to help the Stogs, he wasn't there that day and if I'm being completely honest.... I don't even think that those horrible children ever noticed!

The clock on the wall was the only constant sound that came from the room. Every so often one of the children would make a large sigh or a groan. I honestly don't know if I could tell you if those children learned anything in that class! They just kept themselves to themselves and when they did not, they showed off their true colours. They were not a pretty sight for anyone.

"What time is it?" Grr Lee asked, breaking the silence of the morning. Princess made a snorting sort of sound at the thought of Grr Lee's sort of riff raff even speaking in her presence.

It was followed by the poshest voice you may ever have heard. "When will this day be over? I should be calling Winston right now so that he can come collect me from this dreadful place."

They sat in silence for another few minutes. The clock was too high for Grr Lee's head. He was so heavy that even trying to put up his head was a struggle for him. So, he asked again.

"What time is it?" he said this time with a little bit more confidence to his voice.

"I make it quarter to twelve!" intervened Summer, quite politely.

"Fantastic!" Grr Lee announced gleefully. "Almost time for my third breakfast. Only 10 minutes to kill!"

"Ugh!" Princess responded disgusted. "You disgust me!"

"Actually, I find it quite liberating." Summer paused for a moment whilst she pondered on the next thing to say to someone who obviously did not really care. "Someone expressing themselves not held down by the social constraints of standard mealtimes."

"Oh gosh," Princess whined as she had to listen further to these people constantly bothering her. "When will Winston be here! It's not like we're even learning anything!"

Grr Lee was getting frustrated himself with the constant nagging of Princess. She was often like this. He was hungry and tired of listening to her relentless complaining. "This place is sooo boring!!!" he moaned. "When are we going to do something.... Fun!"

"If only I had my tablet," Princess complained. "I could order Winston to come and pick me up from here! "

They sat in silence for a few moments again before Summer spoke. She was the most eager in the class to learn something and broke the silence again. "Guys!" she announced to everyone, "there's a bunch of books back there! Why don't we try and find something to read about?"

Grr Lee looked over at the books and then looked back to Princess and Summer quite anxiously. He was a boy that had most certainly been given either a mobile phone or electronic device at such a young age that he genuinely had a fear of reading. His mind raced at the horrifically disgusting idea.

"Reading! Really? No streaming of Internet videos, or some gamer howling and screeching as he played video games that looked as if they had been designed by a three-year-old?"

The idea seemed preposterous!

"Fine" resolved Princess, not entirely enthusiastically. "If we must!"

They were just about to slip their chairs out from under their tables when the classroom door slammed open. It was so loud that it made all three of the children jump. Grr Lee let out a yelp like a whimpering puppy. From the corridor, Billy and Mr Pets entered the room.

"Don't touch any of those books!" Billy commanded.

The other three children looked at him bewildered. For a moment, it seemed that none of them actually knew who he was. Even though he had been in the same class as them for several years!

"Is there no teacher for this class?" Mr Pets questioned slightly confused as to why three children would be sitting in a classroom by themselves and not learning anything.

"She went out to get a drink from the water fountain several months ago," replied Princess

Mr Pets stood in silence for a few moments in actual bewilderment that the children would still remain coming to school if the school teacher had made it clear that they had no intention of coming back.

Sumner was the first to question the whole intrusion. "Excuse me, what do you mean don't touch any of those books?" she said it sweetly enough. Although, Mr Pets and Billy hadn't thought about coming up with an excuse.

Billy was not a boy who lied very much and therefore in all honestly told them, "I reckon something's about to happen. Something magical is about to happen."

They all looked at Billy with dumbfounded expressions their faces. Grr Lee was the first to respond. Not the way that a nice child would respond. Which is why when this chapter has ended, I'm sure many of you will be happy that you are not like Grrr Lee.

"I've never heard so much drivel in all my life. Why are you here and why are you holding that ridiculous battered book?" he shouted angrily.

"Yeah! Like, who does he think he is telling us what to do?" Princess followed. "Like, that - is so what - I should be doing!"

"I beg you children. Please listen to the young man," Mr Pets interjected. "All he has come down here to do is to try and make some friends."

The three children laughed maliciously at Mr Pets words. They were not nice children and - this is the part of the story where – they were due to get their just desserts. Grr Lee left his desk and walked slowly over to the small pile of books at the side of the class. Every step was like an earthquake and made the whole classroom shake. There was a genuine fear from Mr Pets that the foundations of the school were going to break.

Grr Lee found his way through some heavy breathing towards the books. He skimmed through the titles with his big, pudgy fingers before announcing, "ah perfect! *The Million Sausages and Their Perfect Breakfasts.*"

Before he could open the book, he looked over at Billy. Within a heartbeat Grr Lee froze, startled for a moment before his beady little piggy eyes even tried to focus on what was happening. The book in Billy's hands was shaking uncontrollably. It was like there was something trying to get out. Grr Lee moved closer towards the Billy. Summer and Princess kept to the other side of the room but were eagled eyed as to what was going on.

Billy released the book and it fell to the floor. Its thud echoed around the room as if the book was heavier than it looked. It continued to shake ferociously before it finally burst open like an explosion. Grr Lee was thrown back to the end of the class room with such force that he crashed against the far wall, almost crushing Summer and Princess. He groaned with pain and opened his eyes to see multiple ball like creatures throwing themselves with such forceful speed against the ceiling, classroom windows and walls before they finally settled on the ground.

Princess squealed repulsively at the dight of the Stog family that had mercilessly entered the real world again. "Oh my gosh!" she screeched in an un-audible tone. "Like, we're under attack from *FROGS!* Call the police! Call the army! Call anyone!"

Billy had read enough of his father's scribblings to know that Stogs – the Stog's Wife in particular – didn't take kind to being insulted. If you or anyone that you know has participated in a "Stupendous Tale of Greatness" or:

- Have been out in a container to be fed to a snake
- Been held captive on a prison ship
- Been insulted by bakers, pirates and some children
- Been transported through several books

... Then you will know how exhausting the whole situation can be. If this hasn't then – speaking as someone that it has happened to – I would not wish the ordeal on anyone. To end such a story on being insulted by a child (who has no regard for anyone else but herself) would have pushed most Stogs over the edge. But not this time...

Upon the Stog's Wife's face was nothing more than relief. She helped her husband up to his feet and they both looked at Billy and Mr Thomas. Billy was ashamed of his actions that had caused the Stogs to end up on the HMS Jolly Roger. He held the book that his father had written tightly but they all knew how dangerous it could be. No one deserved to go through what the Stog family had been through.

Well actually ...

I don't pretend to know what happened that day. I can come up with my assumptions as I'm sure you as the reader can as well. What I like to think that happened was that Billy and Mr Pets took the Stog Family away to safety and realised how much damage such a book could do. They tried to dispose of it in a one of the bins in the school. Following that, I guess you can assume what you want. Perhaps Grrr Lee was looking for some food? Perhaps Summer wanted to find something that she could bring home and add to the collection of other worthless items that was in her caravan? Maybe Princess finally got a hold of Winston and wanted to show her gratitude by getting him a present that she thought was suitable? I don't know and I don't think that any of us will ever know. All I know is that an open book was found in the middle of an empty classroom. On the page that was single drawing of three individuals that looked something a little bit like this:

CHAPTER TWENTY-FIVE

The intention for a closing chapter of any story is for you - the reader - to finish it believing that all the main and sub plot points have been closed and that all the characters introduced have (at some point or another) either developed enough for you to feel as if you've done well investing so much time in them. As the writer, I cannot promise you that this has been accomplished but it's worth giving it a try.

Take the three despicable children for example that billy spent years with trying to make a connection. Sure, their ending was a little vague and maybe not as developed as you'd have hoped but I highly doubt that you thought during their initial introduction that such dire and horrible people would redeem themselves. Some of you would have been impressed that characters who had such little time in the story even got an ending at all. Others would have thought that a more developed ending where it turned out they were all nice children in the end would gave been getter. Maybe it wasn't the perfect ending for them and perhaps even wasn't the right one. But their brief interaction within the story is over.

The fairy tale characters can now be found once again in their stories for future generations to enjoy and learn from. If you go to any children's section in a library, I'm sure you'll find them.

The pig went into a tale where he ventures into newfound independence with his two brothers that he was reunited with. After so long on a prison ship you'd think he was a little bit smarter, but I do recall hearing that he built a home out of straw. For someone so grace and caring in a jail cell he's a little gullible and irresponsible. I wouldn't worry though, I'm certain that there will be no repercussions of him building a house of straw. Especially when his other brothers built homes of sticks and bricks!

The puppet boy also made it back into his own story. He became rather famous and - in 2022 alone -went have three different feature films produced about him and his life. Obviously (for some bizarre reason) his adventures upon the HMS Jolly Roger were not recorded in any of these accounts! At this point, I don't really know what the end of his story turned out to be! However, depending on the iteration that you either read or watched we'll always get a different answer.

The Baker returned home after subjecting the Stog's Wife to Warden Hook and the HMS Jolly Roger. Still dismayed with living so close to fairy tale creatures, he sold his home and moved to Los Angeles to try and make a name for himself as a famous baker. I believe there was a pilot released for a TV show called "Cake or Death" that never really took off. All I know is that you can now find him on the Hollywood Boulevard as one third of the trio BBC (the Butcher, Baker and the Candlestick maker).

Warden Hook and his crew returned to their story as blood thirsty pirates. Warden – or now Captain Hook – restored the Jolly Roger to one of the fiercest pirate ships on the sea returning to the land and sea where children never had to grow up. He and his crew sailed the sea looking to put an end to a much younger Prisoner Pan. Prisoner Pan had once again learned the ability to fly and took joyous pride in being able to carry on the adventures that he had had not been able to under Hook's imprisonment. Although they never spoke about it again, both Hook and Pan were aware that Hook's wish was to restore all of the creatures into their own stories. It may have been out of cowardness, or it may have been Hook seeking redemption, we'll never know. Prisoner Pan may have caused Hook countless trials and escapades since his return into their story however, there would always be an unspoken amount of respect for him for doing the right thing.

As for Mr Pets, his store continued to bring joy to the numerous families that would go in seeking a new family friend. Though he had lived a joyous experience watching parents and children's eyes and hearts open up when they found the right pet, there were rumours in the years to come that he, his family and the pets from the store abandoned the quiet village life and joined a motorcycle gang. But that's a different story for a different time.

As for Billy and the Stogs, well they had become newfound friends. Mr Pets had given Billy the copy that he had found of "The Stog's Wife" so that the Stog family could be safe forever in their own story. They spent one last night together with the children learning about different items that were in a ten-year-olds bedroom. Many of the toys that Billy had were tried out that night for when Alice, Newt and

Scruffball were older to cause havoc in other children's homes; the same way that their parents had done in previous stories before they finally made their way into the safety of the pages of their own book. Billy grew much older and eventually had a family of his own. He kept the book safe for years to come and read it to his own daughter. Never letting on the magic that books have or his own mysterious adventure that he had been on with the Stog family

However, that night the Stog and his wife had stayed out of the pages for a few more hours. It was the last time that all of them were going to be together and so they wanted to end it well. Billy had spoken with his father and they had apologised to each the for the actions that had led them to not speaking for a little while. Mr Thomas then revealed to Billy that he had actually another copy of the book that had been "mysteriously misplaced". Rather than put anyone else through the ordeal that the Stog family had been through, Billy had come up with an idea to finally finish off his father's book without causing too much indifference with the rest of the story.

As I mentioned at the start of this story, one of the things that Hook's crew liked to do was sing songs of galore and silliness. They ensured that the pirates on the Jolly Roger sang the silliest of sings as they set out into the sunset. I believe it went a little bit like this:

"There was a young sailor Willy Jones was his name,
Who played the accordion and searched bars for fame,
He joined with his brother a ship that set sail for sea,

They were the crew of the Jolly Roger sailing ever so free!

It set sail for Scotland in a ship ever so fine,
It carried gold riches and the most expensive wine,
In jail cells with Puppet's and ferocious pigs,
Willy wrote a new song and it's this song he sings!

Yo ho, we'll sail through the see,
A pirate's life for you but oh not for me,
Oh No, it's love song I've smothered,
Or at least I tried to if it weren't for my brother,
Yo ho, its getting cold so wear mittens,
It's not goodbye to you friends, it's simply good riddance!

Willy Jones then realised that he was under a curse,
And that's why this wee shanties ended up worse,
His brothers drunk some rum and offers a bet,
To make this nautical nonsense something ye won't forget,

Willy told him he was writing "Goodbye and Good Riddance,"
Which he thought would be funny if he could rhyme it with
kittens,
Line the words up in order, so the story makes sense.
But will he? Or wont he? It's getting intense!

Yo ho, we'll sail through the sea,
A pirate's life for you but oh not for me,
Oh no, Brother he's mentioned kittens,
It's not goodbye to your money, just simply good riddance!

A third verse for torture and to cause you great pain,

Just reading bad writings driving readers insane,
Willy should have been watching when those rocks up they came,
But the bet cost that whole voyage and the crew cursed his name!!!

Nae ghosts or sea hags or mermaids arrived,
No sign of nae pirates dead or alive,
No golden sea monster with legs eight or ten,
So, let's go to the chorus for that rubbish again!

Yo ho, we'll sail through the see,
A pirate's life for you but oh not for me,
Oh No, it's love song I've smothered,
Or at least I tried to if it weren't for my brother,
Yo ho, its getting cold so wear mittens,
It's not goodbye to you friends, it's simply good riddance!

I know what you're thinking!

"How could a writer have so much insight to what a mischievous little creature got up to in such a "Stupendous Tale Of Greatness"? For this to be such a reliable source, the writer would have had to be there."

Maybe he was. Maybe, the writer was that mischievous little creature throughout the whole thing. Wouldn't that have been cool? That you find out that the Stog had written this whole autobiographical tale? Maybe he went back into his own story and wrote the pages himself just to let you – as the reader - know what great adventures a Stog can really get up to.

Or perhaps not. Maybe this hasn't been a reliable source at all. Maybe it was all nonsense. And perhaps you'll never know!

I did, many many pages ago! I begged and pleaded with you. I begged you to behave. Two stories went by and you saw the disruption that a Stog and his family could cause. Maybe, you were even prepared for the Stog and his family to try and cause havoc in your house going into this story. If the Stog did write this, then he found the perfect way to distract long enough to cause further chaos in your house when you weren't paying attention! I'm sorry, I really am!

The End?

Printed in Great Britain
by Amazon